VIRTUAL REALITY

Flashes of bright color—tropical birds—battered the air within the leaf canopy, with cries that sliced the quiet. Among the pillars padded a silent tiger, crossing from blinding sunlight into shadow and back.

The glowing, enamel-on-black signs that hung high up among the pillars matched the selections on my menu bar. . . .

GLASS HOUSES

LAURA J. MIXON

A TOM DOHERTY ASSOCIATES BOOK
· NEW YORK

GLASS HOUSES

A Tor Book
Published by Tom Doherty Associates, Inc.
175 Fifth Avenue
New York, N.Y. 10010

TOR® is a registered trademark of Tom Doherty Associates, Inc.

Cover art by Tom Canty

ISBN: 0-812-51918-3

First edition: May 1992

Printed in the United States of America

0 9 8 7 6 5 4 3 2 1

For my father, Earl Mixon, with love.

WE PLAY JUNGLE JIM

GETTING Golem up the support structure was slow work with the winds at gale force. I'd hoped to reach the building before Howler Felix hit the coast, but I-Golem wasn't halfway up the scaffolding when hot rain exploded from the low cloud ceiling, pounding Golem's metal shell and blurring my-his vision. The sky spat electricity—mercury-white splashes that strobed the night sky and made the tie cables tremble—and the wind screamed rage till I had to turn the volume down to keep my eardrums from bursting.

This scavenge couldn't wait for better weather. I'd gotten the job by promising Vetch I'd recover the salvage before they knocked the building down, and he doesn't have much patience with complications or delays. And the demolition waldos were due to arrive in the morning.

Golem is oblivious to howler weather. He's too

old and stupid to realize he needs to take it slow on
a climb; my-his linkware is pretty simple-minded.
So I had to use caution for him, my thousand-pound,
titanium/metaceramic scrounge, as I piloted him up
the tie lines and scaffolding that kept the old Chase
Manhattan Bank building from collapsing into the
shipping lanes.

Lightning struck: the trashed-out scraper next
door lit up like an arc welder's rod and the blast
toppled me-Golem. Water rushed up. Then vision
and hearing went out—the blast flung me back to
my own body in my Queens apartment.

"Shit."

I buried fists in the cushioning gel, lurched up
trailing brain web wires, and bashed my forehead on
the lower edge of the control panel. With a grunt I
blinked away tears, fell back into the gel, rubbed my
head. Easy, Ruby, I thought, easy; you won't get
back into Golem's head all junked on adrenaline. I
took some slow, deep breaths.

The air was damp and smelled of ozone, mold,
and Lysol. Felix raged outside my window but didn't
sound as angry as it had to me-Golem, downtown.
Muted by the walls, the wind rumbled, and machine whispers came from the bank of computers
and radio-signal amplifiers crammed onto my book-
shelves.

The entry light cast a crooked yellow trapezoid
across my legs half-buried in the clear gel of the
squish-couch and onto the wood floor. Sheer curtains fluttered above the air conditioner and the mobile above it, a plywood pterandodon skeleton in a
geodesic bamboo cage, turned slowly on its string.
Rodents scratched around in the walls and outside,
fists of rain smashed against the double-paned glass.

Then I noticed that Melissa's chair at the foot of her bed was empty.

"Melissa? Are you home?"

Just to check, even though I already knew. My voice carried around corners and echoed back at me. She'd left.

"Shit," I said again, and flicked at the buttons on the panel. A quick scan of Golem's control lights blinking overhead calmed me—his backup visuals were blank, but he was still functional.

The programming kicked back in then and pulled me back to Golem. I-he looked down into a nasty swirling tumult. His retracted wheel had snagged in a tie cable as he'd pitched over the side, and I-he was hanging upside down like a wrecked car on a magnet, still trying to climb. The headlight mounted between his cameras bounced off cables, water, walls, as I-he flailed, twisting, in the wind. Double images danced and whirled in my head while his camera eyes spun independently on their platforms, the program seeking to restore binocular vision.

I swallowed my heart, which had climbed up into my throat, and overrode his climb-and-swing routine. You stupid fuck. Pathetic monster.

My-his vision—and consequently my stomach—settled. I-he groped back and up for the scaffolding bar. For this scavenge I'd equipped Golem with his largest carrying container, which I call the Coffin because of its size and shape when empty. It's my own design: a metaceramic frame with FlexBind webbing stretched across it. It can hold up to three and a half cubic yards of material in a variety of shapes and sizes. Unfortunately, the Coffin constrains him; none of his arms could reach far enough backward with their hooks or clamps in the right orientation to grasp the cable. Then a flash of light-ning lit up a steel beam directly ahead.

With the caught wheel as a fulcrum I-he used the blasts of wind and cartwheeled his arms to get myself-him swinging in the right direction. His schwarzenegger arm was equipped with the C-hook; at the apex of the swing I-he got the C-hook around the beam, but his wheel twisted free with the mo-tion and I-he skittered a meter or two down the sup-port beam before the C-hook caught on a rivet. I-he slammed into the beam and hung on for dear live-lihood.

A quick systems check: amber needles spread across my-his vision on a cyan grid. No damage. Sturdy Golem. And I could use his telescope arm now.

It took some fumbling to get the fine manipulator off his telescoping extension and the crab claw on. Then I-he extended the arm upward. It telescoped out a good three meters, which was enough, if not for the wind messing up my aim. I-he managed to hook the tie line on the fifth try. Collapsing the telescope extension hauled me-him up—grudgingly, with a mighty groaning of servos. But the servos held.

Useless old thing. Serve you right if you did fall two hundred feet into a flood.

I-he renewed his grip on the tie cable with one of his two finger-handed arms. After securing him I let him dangle like an old gorilla while I-he took a look around. The building was much closer than I'd re-alized: a looming blackness that filled up my-his sight and, when lightning struck, reflected the storm in its metal struts and broken windows.

DATA SCAVENGE

BOMBINGS had rendered the scraper's interior as fragile as eggshells. Wind howled through the fire-charred rooms and corridors, whipping up devils of dirt, fog, steam, and papers; great holes gaped in the floors and walls. I-Golem shone his light through a hole in the floor and saw splashing water far below. The building trembled and moaned like it was afraid.

Vetch had given me several electronic maps of the building interior, but they were outdated and fragmented; it took hours to navigate through the ruined building and locate the vault. The data's owner had lost the locking code, which made things tougher—it took me-Golem maybe another couple of hours to cut into the steel wall and repower the archaic lock, break the code, and open the door.

Tens of thousands of laser disks lined the vault's data storage shelves. Many of the disks were damaged and all of them were coated in dust. I-Golem scooped them up with his spatulate arm and then, using his finger-handers—his most humanlike arms with their eight mutually opposable fingers—packed them in gelpaper. Then I-he loaded up the Coffin.

After flipping the Coffin over, I-Golem retracted his wheels, which put me-him on his back, and rolled myself-him over the Coffin's skids. Once upright I checked his macroscale: over two and a half metric tons of goods, the readout said. Vetch would be one happy junk nazi.

Golem's never been rated, so I don't know what ASTM would say his heaviest safe load was. But I'd loaded him this heavy before. It was the weight in combination with howler Felix, the building's condition—and the climb down—that scared me. The walls trembled with each blast of wind and caused chalky plaster to cascade from the ceiling. I had the sense that the walls bowed inward—as if a giant hand were squeezing the building, trying to crush it.

To give Golem added stability I extended and dropped onto the set of smaller, auxiliary wheels at the top of Golem's chassis. Then, keeping close to the edges of rooms, I-he headed outward, and I tried to keep my mind off the blasts of wind, the trembling walls, and the groaning struts.

I EXPERIENCE ENVIE

AT first I thought the man was a pile of rubbish, when Golem's light struck him. Then I-Golem saw his eyes glint.

I-Golem rolled forward and reared, Kodiak-like, to get a better view. The glint vanished—the man had closed his eyes, trying to hide. I-Golem activated the speaker.

"Come on out," I-he said, but was drowned out by an explosion of thunder: the building rocked, and plaster fell all around.

"Come on out," I-Golem said again. "I know you're there."

After a pause, some of the layers of paper and

Sheetrock fell away, and a face peered out at me-Golem, blinking in Golem's spotlight. I-he retracted the auxiliary wheels, dimmed the light, and supplemented my-his vision with the infrared processors.

"What are you doing here?" I-Golem asked.

"I might ask the same of you."

His voice was baritone and melodic with an accent—maybe French or Spanish. The black skin of his face, beaded with sweat, had deep creases. Golem has no tactile temperature sense—only sight with IR, sound, and a sense of touch which is merely pressure against his metal skin—so it took me a moment to figure out the old man must be sweating from the heat.

His close-cropped hair was so pure a white that it looked like a haze of cotton batting. Enormous diamonds encrusted the curves of his ears and the infrared plume above his head told me he wore a cool suit.

Bif bam pow. My muscles spasmed with the shock like he'd thrown cold water on me, and Golem twitched in sympathy.

"You're an envie!"

"You needn't worry." He stood, brushing the debris from himself and clutching a brown gelpaper envelope close to his chest like it was something valuable. His cool suit's pattern changed through a series of luminous Celtic knots in greys, beige, and blues on a background of dull umber. Tasteful, if a bit boring. "I shan't report you."

His gaze was as cool and remote as a fish's eyes, but I figured he must be nervous, thinking I was a refugee or a renegade soldier with a stolen waldo.

"I'm licensed, pal. I built this unit myself and he's one-hundred-percent environmentally sound, recycled materials. I have the receipts to prove it. So what are you going to report me for—bad taste?"

He looked me-Golem up and down, but didn't say anything. I doubt he could see well enough with the light in his eyes exactly how ugly my Golem was. I half expected him to ask for my license number. But he must have seen enough to figure out Golem wasn't pilfered government issue, because he released a breath and wiped away sweat, and rubbed his haze of hair. The floor trembled beneath a dull rumble. Felix was getting angrier still.

"What are you doing here?" I-Golem asked. "This building is condemned. You could get hurt."

A pained smile came onto his lips. "I assure you, madam, it was never my intent to come here." He limped over to a broken chair propped against a collapsed desk and sat down. Golem's light tracked him. His chest rose and fell, rose and fell. "I was shipwrecked."

"How did you get up here?"

"I climbed."

I couldn't help myself. I laughed. Golem's transmitter broadcast a metallic ratcheting sound. "In this howler? It's got to be at least a six-pointer."

His eyes glinted at me-Golem again but he stayed silent. Maybe he'd climbed up before the storm had hit; the wind had been churning the water up for a full day ahead of time, so it was possible. But he didn't say so and I could tell I'd annoyed him.

Another spasm rippled through the building—I-Golem rolled sideways and slammed into a wall and the old man toppled with a cry. I-Golem did a drunken little dance till I got his gyros steadied. On the floor, the old man was groaning. He clutched at his leg, the one he'd been limping on.

"My knee . . . I sprained it climbing."

That didn't look so good. We were almost a hundred and fifty feet above the south Manhattan dikes. Even if the weather hadn't been so bad, he couldn't climb down on that leg. And he must weigh over two hundred pounds, with the cool suit on. This could really screw up my scavenge. I sighed.

"Well, come on." I-Golem opened the chest cavity and unfurled a FlexBind web which I usually used to carry groceries or, occasionally, small scavenges. I'd ridden in it myself and even carried Melissa once. It'd hold a large adult like him, though not comfortably. "We'd better get us both out of here."

He still didn't say anything for a minute. Then, with a grunt, he came to his feet.

"I am indebted to you," he said. He unzipped his cool suit and tucked his packet inside, then limped over. I-Golem extended an arm to give him a boost and stretched the netting out with the telescope arm.

Then a blast—thunder at close range—deafened us. A traveling wave surged through the floor and up the walls. I-Golem and the old man went down. A rumbling swelled like the brassy noise of an oncoming train, metal screamed, and several hundred tons of steel, concrete, and plaster collapsed on top of us.

MAN SCAVENGE

I don't know if you've ever had a skyscraper collapse on you. I don't recommend it. The floor gave out under me, cascades of concrete and steel fell onto my head, the screams of the old man filled my ears like someone was murdering him. I remember those few seconds in flashes, like it all happened under strobe lights.

His nearness to me-Golem when the ceiling collapsed was the only thing that kept him from being killed instantly. One of Golem's arms crocked up as I-he toppled over and protected the old man's head and upper chest. The old man probably wished he was dead, though, because a steel beam fell across his abdomen and crushed his internal organs and let buckets of blood spill into his abdominal cavity.

I know all this because I-Golem wasn't completely disabled in the crush. The same steel beam that fell on the old man lodged against the wall and kept other chunks of mass from destroying Golem's casing. That much I saw before the shock threw me home.

I struggled backward through the gel to the wall, pulled my knees to my chest, and shook. The connector dangled from wires in my hand—I must have pulled it loose from the beanjack at my crown. I wanted to tear the monofilaments right out of my brain. But the old man's screams hung in my ears. He was still alive in there and he wouldn't be for long. No waldo rescue squad, no ambulance would get there in time to save him. Every second counted. So I went back.

Golem's light had gotten smashed and the infrared was useless in that chaos. Systems weren't in great shape—the needles danced like amber Pick-Up Stix in my-Golem's vision. Four of his eight giga-crystals were shattered. Besides the arm immobilized over the old man's head, two limbs were inoperable, crushed. One of his two cameras was out, too. His chassis was severely damaged, with hydraulic pressure dribbling slowly away.

It took only seconds to clear out all the software and fill the remaining four linkware crystals with the bare-bones operating systems. The gyros told me which way was up, so I knew which way to dig, and I-Golem had length and strength—of the two of Golem's five arms still working, one was his telescope arm and the other his schwarzenegger. I've scavenged under rubble before and I know how to keep an unstable structure from collapsing. Things didn't seem too bad, except for the old man's screaming. So I-Golem got started.

He was crazy with pain. A couple of times I-Golem tried to comfort him but he didn't listen. It finally got to me—I-he yelled at the old man to shut the fuck up and stop feeling sorry for himself. Like he didn't have a reason. Christ. I hope he was too far gone to understand.

Anyhow, as the sounds he made got wetter and softer I-Golem dug faster. But he'd been silent for what seemed like days before Golem's hole saw drilled through to air. That give me-him enough light to see how to work free.

My-Golem's ultrasound filaments fractured the chunk of concrete that had Golem pinned against

the steel beam. Then I-he—ever so carefully!—
disconnected the arm that protected the old man's
head, rolled myself-Golem all the way onto his back,
then retracted the wheels—which lifted me-Golem
up and gave the wheels purchase on the floor on
either side of the Coffin—and slid myself-him off of
it. With some judicious shoving and wedging I-he
freed myself-him from the debris. Then I-Golem
propped up wreckage, cleared a path for the old man,
and slid him free.

I saw then that there was no point in calling an
ambulance. His body was already starting to cool. I
could have used Golem's IR earlier, after all, and
saved myself a lot of work.

I still remember all the details—the expression
he'd died with; the way his crushed arm got left
behind; the way his belly had swollen up with blood
till it looked like the belly of a tick.

Anyhow, I sat there, squatting inside my battered
Golem, and looked at him for a while till I realized
that the sun had risen and was shining into Golem's
camera. Beyond the crumbled wall, where another
interior room had been last night, was open air and
twisted snarls of metal struts. I-Golem caught a
glimpse of the Manhattan-Queens ferry moving up
the sparkling East River, trailed by crying gulls; last
night's gales had softened to a breeze. Streamers of
clouds raced inland overhead.

The storm remediation waldos, hundred-foot-tall
mantises with blue flashing lights and steel maws,
crawled along the streets below, lifting wreckage
and debris with their crane arms. They scooped
sludge and wood with their dozer mouths, dropping
the debris into the massive hoppers they dragged
behind.

According to Golem's chronometer, it was almost

six. The building wrecker waldos were due—we had to get out.

There wasn't much hope for the scavenged data but I-Golem checked the Coffin anyway. As I'd suspected, they were so much worthless debris, bent and broken. Man, was Vetch going to be pissed. He hated losing salvage.

I-Golem emptied the Coffin, put the old man inside, and slid the Coffin onto Golem's back. Then I-Golem and the old man headed for the nearest support cable.

A failed scavenge, a failed rescue, and Melissa off fucking some strange man for spending money in the middle of a hurricane. All in all, not a good night.

POPCORN, BEER, AND
COPS IN THE JELLY

No, he didn't tell me who he was—he said he was shipwrecked. I don't know how he got up there; he said he climbed. No, I can't substantiate my story with Golem's CASC memory because half of his gigacrystals were destroyed and I had to wipe out everything but the essentials to get us down the scaffolding.

Cops never believe you; they think if they stick you in a bare room with metal-reinforced glass on the windows and yell the same question fifty times you'll slip up or crack under the pressure and yell, "All right, I confess. I dropped a skyscraper on the old fart!"

Of course, I had the advantage over them, because

they had to crane their necks up all eight feet of Golem to make eye contact. And it was eye contact with a machine, not with me. I'd disconnected from the beanjack and was maintaining contact via the jellovision tube and the radio link, so I could sit drinking a beer and eating plantain chips and watch them from my own comfy squish-couch.

So it'll come as no surprise that they didn't like how I'd piloted my waldo to the station instead of coming in person. But when I pointed out that a) I couldn't very well carry the body myself and couldn't pilot Golem and report *in corpus*, too, and b) they had my name, license number, personal contact number, debit account numbers, and home address, so I wasn't exactly out of reach, the lieutenant shrugged and dropped the subject.

Golem was probably my best corroboration, though. He looked even more like a heap of junk than usual, and kept dripping hydraulic fluid and dropping bits of metal and metaceramic all over their linoleum—causing the housekeeping robot no end of distress, I'm sure.

They finally went away and left Golem alone. I turned his volume up so I'd know if someone came into the precinct interrogation room and left him dormant while I went to the bathroom. I even had time to pop some popcorn and finish most of another beer.

I came back into the room when the door back at the precinct opened. Beer in hand, I sank into the gel of my couch and flipped a switch on the pull-down control panel to reactivate Golem. His camera swiveled and focused on the woman who moved into range and solidified inside the jello-tube. She must have been a cop but she didn't look like one. She was somewhere in her forties, with dark skin and a large nose, shoulder-length silver hair swept back from her face—and dressed in the baggy veils, wraps, and gauze that *natureils* wear.

I don't know why that shocked me, that a cop could be a *natureil*. You could classify Melissa and me that way, too, but we couldn't afford any part of the envie life-style much less own our own environment suits, so we didn't exactly have a choice, and she did.

She buried her hands halfway up to the elbows in her baggy pants pockets and looked right up into Golem's camera. I got a chill, like she could see me through the camera.

"I'm Sheila Nanopoulos, the precinct captain." She paused but I didn't fill in the gap, so she continued. "All this questioning might be frustrating for you, Ms. Kubick, after your good-faith attempt to rescue Dr. Nasser. But when someone dies under unusual circumstances we must investigate."

Someone who matters, you mean, I thought; if Melissa or I were killed it'd be days before anyone noticed, and hell would freeze over before anyone would spend money to find out how or why.

"Sure," I said. "I understand that."

"Good. Then I hope you'll understand that since the building where Dr. Nasser died is already under deconstruction your—'Golem', is it?—"

A knot formed in my throat and I went cold all over. I rubbed my arms. "Yes."

"—your Golem is currently the only remaining physical evidence from the scene of Dr. Nasser's death. We'll have to impound your waldo, for a short time, to confirm your story."

"You mean you want to make sure Golem isn't a murder weapon," I said. She gave me a long, appraising look.

"You're not being accused of murder, Ms. Kubick. If everything you told us was true our forensic work will be simply a formality and your waldo will be returned to you within a day or two. If we find any anomalies, of course, we'll have to investigate further, and it might take longer."

"Oh," I said, and shoved down, hard, on this sudden desire that surged up, to scream in her face, to encircle her wrinkled old throat with Golem's crab claw and choke her.

"Ma'am," I managed, after I'd gotten control of myself, "Golem is my only source of income. I lost tens of thousands of dollars' worth of salvage trying to rescue the old man, and repairing Golem will take almost that much. If you keep him for too long I won't be able to pay my bills and I could end up out on the street."

"We'll be as quick as we can, I assure you. If everything is in order, you should have your Golem back by Friday."

It was Wednesday. Surely I could hold the landlord off for a few more days. Barring "anomalies."

"Thank you, ma'am. I appreciate that." I popped open the control panel on Golem's side. She pulled an override crystal from her pocket and moved out of the range of his damaged vision. Then my jellotube filled with milky smoke and all the lights on the control panel above eye level went from green and yellow to red. I sat there in the dimness looking at the jello-tube with a warm, sweaty beer in my hand, tears in my eyes, and a knot of futile anger in my belly.

They were going to make me a scapegoat. The old man was an envie, obviously an important one, and I wasn't much higher in status than a refugee. His family was going to be angry, and I was an easy target.

So the fact that on the way to the First Precinct station I'd taken his diamonds from his ears and the brown gelpaper envelope from his envie cool suit, made a detour to hide them, and then wiped Golem's memory of it, was probably one of the riskiest things I could ever have done. But the old man's family was too wealthy to miss a few stones, and if I could ride out this storm those diamonds meant Melissa and I would be set for life. Never mind whatever was in that envelope.

I Break the Breakage
News to Vetch

Vetch didn't handle it as well as I'd hoped, and that's saying something.

"You trashed the disks? You trashed the *disks*?" He repeated it several times, as his face slowly darkened in my jello-tube. I was afraid he'd pop.

"I told you, there was nothing I could do. The building collapsed. The salvage got trashed. Sorry."

"Nothing you could do? Nothing you could do."

"Would you stop repeating everything I say? You sound like an echo."

"Of all the people I could have hired, I picked you." He shook his head with a bitter laugh. "You're a fuck-up, Kubick, a world-class fuck-up. I had a data trader ready to pay me fifty-two thousand dollars—minimum—for those laser disks!"

I chewed my lip. When Vetch goes ballistic he sounds just like my dad and it gives me a queasy feeling in my gut. "What do you want me to do? I can't bring the data back."

And I'd thought he was going to explode before. He went beet-colored and sputtered for a minute or so. Then he leaned forward and said in a low, mean voice, "Then you better find a way to make up for this fuck-up."

"It wasn't my fault!"

"I don't care whose fault it was—you'll pay me every fucking dollar of that fifty-two grand or I'll be in your face so bad you won't even be able to wipe your ass without me knowing how many squares you used."

"Gosh, say what you really mean. Don't hold it in."

"I mean it. You pay me damages or I'll find a way to hurt you and that's a promise."

"Damn you, Vetch, we signed a no-fault contract and you know it."

But he'd already disconnected. I wanted to throw my beer at the empty jello-tube, but that would have been a waste of good beer.

MORE NEWS BREAKAGE

I didn't dare go to the cache. I didn't even feel safe making a run to the corner deli for groceries. I ought to have tuned in to Master Cho's Street-Defense and Aero-Art Exercise Hour and done my usual work-out, and then slept; my habit is to work out for an hour when the show comes on at 2:30 P.M. and then shower and sleep from four or five P.M. till midnight. That way I can use the cool hours to go out, if the need should arise.

But I was too restless to exercise and not even remotely sleepy. I kept seeing that old man dead, no diamonds in his ears. I could get on the nets; *virtu* beat the hell out of its poorer relation, jellovision— but the access beanie I had was an illegal one, a blink beanie. And I half expected the police to burst in with a search warrant any minute. The last thing I needed was to be caught stealing time from the nets. So I just sat drinking beer in the apartment till way past my bedtime, not-watching jellovision, starting at strange noises until the beer shrank my event horizon to the point where I didn't care, and waited for Melissa to come back.

But when loud voices started downstairs and a battery of footsteps clattered up the stairwell I could tell this time was different. My skin started to creep up the back of my neck like it wanted to hide on top of my head and at the knock on the door I jumped with a squeak of sheer terror. I got up and ran to the window.

That candy-apple-red electric collovehicle outside my window, three stories below, was no police van. It had a thicket of antennae, a radio dish, and polarized windows, and was double-parked in the abandoned, midafternoon street amid mounds of trash and overturned, burnt-out wrecks. I couldn't see the lettering on the sides, but the van had to belong to reporters.

The knock came again. I crept up to the door and peered through the peephole. Two strange men stood there, one tall and one short, decked out in waxed ringlets and glowing art-deco cool vests, both with netlink headsets and the tall one with a shoulder cam. Definitely reporters.

Gathered around them were half the inhabitants
of the building, all of them jabbering, pointing, and
elbowing each other. And standing at the front of
the crowd was Darian Vetch, standing there with
his hairless chest smeared with a cubist's abstrac-
tion in sunscreen paints, his cape and baggy pants
of reflective silver and his net specs perched on his
nose with the earset dangling around his neck. Either he'd slipped inside with the reporters, or maybe
one of the junkies let him in. So much for a quiet
day at home alone.

I pressed my ear to the door. A muffled, unfamil-
iar voice said, "Looks like she's not in."

"Oh, she's there, all right." That was Vetch. "She
never goes out. She rob somebody besides me?"

"She's a real hero." It was the same voice that had
wondered if I wasn't in. "What's her name, Terry?"
And in a louder voice, "Open up, Ms. Kubick.
Please. My name is Peter Corbin and this is Terence
Fielder. We're reporters with WYZE. We want to
talk to you about what happened this morning in
south Manhattan."

If Vetch hadn't been there I'd probably have just
waited till the reporters went away. Considering
what I'd done with the earrings and envelope, I was
inclined to keep a low profile. But seeing Vetch,
more often my competitor in the junk salvage business than an employer, reminded me that an ap-
pearance on a major local news show would be great
for business. And considering my circumstances, a
little favorable publicity was definitely in order.
Vetch couldn't make too big a scene with all those
people there so I couldn't see how it would hurt.

I pulled the door open with a shaking hand and a
phony smile just as the reporters were about to turn
away.

"Mr. Corbin, Mr. Fielder. Come right in."

They came inside. I tried to shut the door on Vetch when he, and half the building's tenants, tried to follow. His hand went out and stopped the door.

"I'm going to tell these reporters the whole story of how you ripped me unless you pay up right now."

"Go do something useful. Like read the contract." I shoved hard, and, thank you epinephrine, managed to get the door closed before he could shove his way in.

A GIANT OF OUR TIME

SUSAN the anchorwoman spoke. "The early police reports have been verified. A veritable giant of our time, Dr. Youhanna Nasser, died in a collapsed building when Hurricane Felix hit the coast last night. I'm switching to our man on the scene for an update. Peter?"

"Here, Susan." My jello-tube split in half, and an image of Corbin coalesced beside Susan. It had been less than an hour since he and the cam-man had left (dodging Darian Vetch the whole way down the stairs, I might add. I give them credit for being good judges of character). In fact, they must still have been downstairs, since I recognized several of my neighbors in the background, standing on the stoop behind Corbin or peering out the apartment building's front door.

"Dr. Nasser," Corbin said, "the famed philanthropist, one of America's wealthiest men and a political power-behind-the-scenes who twice during his lifetime was named 'Man of the Year' by *Time* Magazine, died last night or early this morning. The cause of death at this point—and I want to stress that no official reports have been released—but the cause of death appears to have been a tragic accident caused by the hurricane.

"Members of the family could not be reached for comment, and we haven't been able to learn what he was doing at sea in hurricane winds, but we have an exclusive on how he died. In this ghetto tenement lives an unlikely hero: Ruth Kubick—"

"That's *Ruby*, damn it," I said. So much for drumming up new business.

"—who was the last person to see Dr. Nasser alive." He shifted and gestured over his shoulder at my apartment building. "Ruth Kubick lives in this ramshackle tenement and ekes out an existence as a waldo wrangler, performing hazardous salvage jobs. Here's the story of how Dr. Nasser died."

They then flashed back and forth between the interview with me and a much-compressed, computer-generated reenactment of the incident, with my voice-over. I had left out the part about the envelope and diamond posts, of course.

A word to the wise. Never watch yourself on the news. In the few glimpses that appeared in the tube, the apartment looked like a roach-infested dump. Which it is, but you don't want strangers thinking so. And my side of the room looked like somebody's garage filled with electronic clutter. In the foreground I sat facing Mr. Suave-and-Relaxed Peter Corbin, dressed in spud rags, perched as stiffly on the edge of the squish-couch as if my spine had fossilized. They'd given me a couple of minutes to freshen up but it would have taken an hour, a professional makeup artist and a whole new wardrobe to make me look like something other than the scruffy, rather malnourished beanhead that I am.

Worse, in every shot they flashed of me, I either stared and said nothing or talked way too fast, giggled nervously, and in general sounded incoherent and inane. The beers I'd drunk didn't help me come across too well, either.

Awful? It was worse than awful. I was thankful most of my acquaintances don't watch the news.

As for the reenactment—their projections of me and Nasser were so accurate they must have violated a host of right-to-privacy laws. It was so convincing I about climbed out of my skin when the concrete and steel started to crumble.

Then, blessedly, the reenactment and my voice and face went away. Susan's face appeared beside Peter's in the tube.

"What a terrible death. Have the police released an official confirmation?"

"No they haven't, Susan, though anonymous police sources support some crucial details, such as the waldo's apparent capabilities and the nature of the injuries Dr. Nasser sustained. Sources say a full police investigation is likely, including an autopsy, since the death was so unusual."

Susan cocked her head, listening; then her expression brightened. "Ah!—Peter, we have Dr. Thomas Chien."

The head and shoulders of a heavyset, fortyish man filled the jellovision, looking rather ill at ease, with a string of words below: *Dr. Thomas Chien, Forensics Expert, Los Angeles CA.*

"Thanks for being with us on such short notice, Dr. Chien. Perhaps you could comment on the nature of Dr. Nasser's death."

"Glad to. As I understand it, death was caused by massive internal hemorrhaging—"

Then his image winked out. "Thank you, Dr. Chien. Peter?"

"The irony, Susan, is that if Ruth Kubick had discovered him only moments earlier she might have saved him. Instead she failed tragically, and Dr. Youhanna Nasser, one of the wealthiest and most powerful men in the nation, died."

And a tragic failure, too, I thought. I popped the top on another sweaty beer and raised it to Peter Corbin as his face faded from the tube. If this newscast is any indication, my friend, you aren't exactly Pulitzer-grade material yourself.

They replaced Susan with a cube shot of the old man in the top of the jello-tube and in the lower left flashed a collage of his speeches and acts with a music overlay. On the lower right, they wove a speech cut out of the words of several important people. Even the President. That impressed me.

And looking at that rich old man's face while everyone said nice things about him I started to feel a little choked up. Which was dumb. He had been as ruthless as he was wealthy and powerful, I was sure, and besides, I didn't even know the man.

"Good-bye, Youhanna Nasser," Susan the anchor-woman said finally. "The world will be a poorer place without you."

Which, with any luck, wouldn't be true for Melissa and me.

FINERY, SPIKES,
AND SILENCE

SHE came home shortly after six, in her spikes and lace and her sequined finery, looking like absolute hell with her black hair messy and her bird-face paint all smudged and sweat-streaked, and flipped on the entry-hall light, which hurt my eyes.

"Turn off the fucking light," I said. She walked past with a bag of groceries and disappeared into the kitchenette, leaving the hall light on.

"Don't be such a bitch."

Pieces of her—elbows, buttocks, feet, and calves—moved in and out of view as she put the groceries away, and then I heard her banging around washing dishes. Most of those were mine. But there only a few, not enough to make a big deal over. Damn it.

She came out with a diet soda under her arm, unwrapping a hero sandwich from its waxed paper. She dug a book out from the shelf, turned on the cone lamp over the lounge lizard at the foot of her bed, kicked off her fuck-me pumps, and then unbuckled the spikes from her forearms and dropped them on the floor. Folding her long legs up like pretzel sticks, she stuck her face into the book.

That was it. No "where's Golem?" No "how was your day?" No nothing. And I sat there staring at her with all the words locked in my throat and tried to figure out how things could get so bad between two people who loved each other.

CRAZY MIKEY SCRAPES
THE PAINT OFF

MELISSA went to bed around 7:30 P.M. She was snoring in minutes. I went to bed about the same time, but couldn't sleep too well despite the lateness of the hour. I tossed and turned and watched the blinking neon colors from the street turn the room inside out, back and forth, like a chameleon, in counterpoint to Melissa's snores.

Around nine o'clock I got up, peed, and got a glass of water. I sat down on the edge of my bed and drained the glass of warm, murky water and then set the glass on the floor and beat up my pillow.

The air seemed even hotter and mustier than usual. Street noises had started outside the window; the night people were getting up and about. The air conditioner started to make a soft thumping noise—probably trying to convince me it was doing its job. I didn't buy it; I'd take the cheap little pecker apart tomorrow anyhow, and check the compressor and the ammonia pressure.

The thumping grew louder, though, and became the sound of blades beating the air. A chorus of shouts rose from the neighborhood kids outside. I knew who it had to be but got up anyway and shoved the curtains aside for a look.

Up the street, Mikey the crazy Texan was taking his antique bubble-glass helicopter for a spin. The copter swayed from side to side, dipping close enough to the building walls to scrape flakes of paint off. It made the hair stand out on my neck just to watch.

Mikey was a competitor and sometime client/ employer, like Vetch, only much higher on the evolutionary scale. He owned a junkyard and I occasionally sold junk to him when I couldn't find a retail customer to pay for a scavenge. He also laid claim to a "shuttle service" but as far as I knew no one would be caught dead in a bird with him.

Sure enough, his curly head of hair was alone in the cockpit when he swooped past my window. The lunatic. I waved but he didn't see me.

I went to bed wearing a smile. He hadn't been out in a while. Well, I had an excuse to go see him, now; I could pay his junkyard a visit and pick up some parts for Golem.

THE SCREAMER

I came awake again when the red LCDs on the jellophone clock were blinking 10:36 P.M., to the sound of a scream on the faintest edge of hearing. The hairs on the back of my neck rose and I sat up clutching the sheet, straining to hear. I couldn't be sure; it was so faint. The muffled traffic sounds and voices outside made it hard to tell—but no, I was sure someone was screaming.

Sleep, Ruby, I told myself. The cops don't give a damn what happens on the fringes of the envies' civilization, and what could I do alone? But the distant scream went on and on till I couldn't ignore it anymore, up and down like the wail of someone in terrible pain and fear. I finally threw the sheet off and padded over in my big T-shirt to look out the window.

The banner boards overhead blinked bright colors,

moving eyes and mouths, slogans and ads. Ugly orange
light from the streetlamps three floors below bounced
off of concrete, water-filled gutters, piles of trash, fire
hydrants, walls soaked in graffiti scrawls. Groups of people stood on the sidewalk and others walked past the
hawkers and vendors with their card tables and trinket-
covered blankets. One and all ignored the screamer.

In a fit of disgust I threw the locks back and jerked
the window upward. Wet heat swallowed me whole;
I stuck my head out and inhaled searing, liquid air
that smelled faintly of trash and urine. The scream
drowned in a swell of human voices, laughter, tires
on pavement, horns honking, and the barking of dogs.

I strained and listened, tried to sift through the
threads of noise. No scream. So I slid the window
shut. And the scream started again.

My hand on the glass pane, I paused, listening to
be absolutely sure. I wasn't, but slid the window open
anyway. The scream stopped again, swallowed by
street noise.

With a curse, I slammed the window shut and
locked it. Melissa muttered something but I ignored
her, threw myself back into bed, and buried my face
in a pillow. I shouldn't have been able to hear much
of anything after that but I still could have sworn
the screamer was out there somewhere.

You know, Ruby, a little voice in my head said,
the nets are active twenty-four hours a day. And you
have a blink-beanie hidden beneath the bed. . . .

But that stupid blink-beanie was one of the reasons Melissa and I were behind on the rent. I'd been
using it way too much instead of hustling for salvage jobs. And if I kept using it so much one of
these days network security was going to catch me.
No blink-beanie, Ruby. No.

I must have fallen asleep finally.

SHE LOVES ME

WHEN Melissa woke up she stretched and smiled her sweet, sleepy child's smile at me, and I was sober by then and in a little better mood. So I made scrambled Eggcels on bagels with hot, spiced kaffe, and we ate breakfast on her bed.

I told her what happened. I left out the part about the diamonds and the envelope; I didn't want to get her in trouble, too.

She went pale and covered her mouth. Her eyes got wide. "They took Golem? Ruby, what will we do? Calen said he'd kick us out if we don't pay the back rent by Monday."

I took her hand. I thought about the plastic baggy she had hidden beneath the floorboards under her bed, stuffed with bills, that she thought I didn't know about. I had a way to earn money; she didn't, except for spreading her legs. If anything ever happened to me she'd need every penny. I couldn't ask her to touch that money.

"It'll be OK," I said. "I'll think of something."

She seemed reassured; she lay her head in my lap and let me stroke her hair.

THE SCREAMER RETURNS

MELISSA finally dragged herself out of bed around 3:00 A.M., showered, and decked herself out. She left, saying she should be back before noon.

The jellovision—or, more exactly, a historical epic comedy, a space opera, some game shows, and the news—kept me company all day.

I kept thinking about the blink-beanie. Facing into the nets was a far more interesting way to spend the day than staring at the jello-tube. And with the blink-beanie it didn't cost a cent.

Vetch had talked me into taking the blind link-ware beanie as payment for a salvage I'd done for him one time, and it was worth a fortune on the shadow market. Looking back, that deal was probably a mistake because if I ever got caught with it I'd be in deep shit, which was why Vetch had palmed it off on me, I'm sure. But it was a decision I couldn't bring myself to regret. If you've ever linked to the nets you'll know what I mean.

At about four P.M. I gave up waiting for Melissa, turned off the JV and the lights, and plugged in my water code at the shower-head panel. I blew the bulk of my week's ration of nonpotable water on a long, warm, luxurious shower, and soaped, rinsed, shampooed, rinsed, shampooed again. Sheer, luxurious glory.

After dripping dry, I lingered over the baby powder and lotions and brushes and such. Almost an hour later I stepped into the main room naked and feeling great. Then I caught a glimpse of myself in Melissa's full-length mirror, which stood on a stand between her chair and her bed. A memory of me from the interview overlaid itself on my mirror image.

I grimaced and with a sigh, ran hands over my breasts and torso, thinking about how full and round Melissa's tits were. And her buttocks. The rough spots on my fingers and palms caught on my skin: all the lotion in the world couldn't make my hands as soft as Melissa's. Her skin was softer than kitten fur or satin. What a fine body she had.

The woman in the mirror frowned at me. Stop thinking about it, I told the image, and turned from the mirror. So I wouldn't have Melissa's snoring to keep me company tonight. So what. I didn't need her around all the time.

I pulled my big T-shirt on, crawled into bed, and pulled the sheet up. Either the shower had over-cooled me or the air conditioner was doing its job too well tonight; goose bumps rose along my arms and legs from the damp chill. I curled up and tucked my hands between my thighs. It got noisy as groups of people walked by underneath the window, talking loudly. One group might have been fighting. I kept expecting the screamer, but there was no screaming, then.

At 10:48 P.M. when I woke up from a dream, though, I heard it: a sorrowful wail rising and falling beneath the street noise. It made my skin creep to listen to it. I tried to ignore it but the scream kept up.

After a good hour of that I decided, screw Vetch and screw the screamer. Tossing the covers off, I scrambled out of bed and dragged the wood crate out from under it. A jumble of wire coil and old electronic parts filled the crate. I dumped them and sprang the hidden catch with a needle wrench, then removed the false bottom and lifted out the blink-beanie. It took only seconds to adjust the settings inside the beanie and reset the switches on my transmission equipment on the control panel.

If you didn't look inside the beanie you'd think it was a bicycle helmet. It's made of Kevlar with rows of red LCDs for decoration, a chin strap, and a bean-link with its own CPU inside the crown. It looked just like an ordinary beanie, in short, and there was no need to hide it. I was just a little paranoid about it, I guess. It fit on with a click that I felt in my skull and jaw rather than heard.

The blind linkware combines a number of hack-ing and mimicry routines to infiltrate network in-formation systems without a charge to any of my accounts. In a while net security would catch up and the beanie would be obsolete, but in the mean-time it's a great invention even if it is a form of theft. I probably shouldn't have used it but since it was the only way I'd ever get to access the nets I did anyhow, when no good movies were in the JV.

I sank into the gel of the couch and buckled the chin strap. A tiny, disembodied caricature of a hand with a pointing forefinger floated at arm's length before me: virtual touch. The virtual-voice icon, which looked like a Barbie-doll-sized megaphone, and a miniature keyboard icon floated on either side of the hand-with-finger icon, shaded. Below them, a red 3 was blinking on the five-level help bar.

The hand-with-finger icon I left in glow-mode. The keyboard icon lit up when I touched it and a full-sized, virtual QWERTY keyboard appeared be-neath my hands. It was a cartoon-looking board with both a numeric and a functional keypad, made of keys as big as antique pennies that floated in air, boxed by fiber-optic threads and bracketed by two floating joysticks. Then I touched the megaphone and it started to glow, with wavy lines coming out of it. The icons and keys felt like crispy cotton balls.

"Thank you," said a disembodied Kurzweil voice. "Virtual interact modes modified. Voice, keyboard, and touch responses now active. Please choose help level from the numbers listed, by touch or voice."

"Help level one, please. And load GridLink."

The icons and words faded. Music swelled in my ears, a chimy GridLink signature tune. A menu bar—five words made of shiny blue letters—appeared overhead at arm's length:

COMMAND   FILE   CONNECT   UTILITIES   MACRO

You could tell that GridLink was a more sophisticated software package: the floating letters were as real as reality gets. They looked cut from blocks and painted with enamel. The only way I could tell they weren't real was that the reflection of the words, like the keyboard, didn't appear in front of my reflection in Melissa's framed mirror.

I reached toward CONNECT and my fingers slid across slippery, cold surfaces. The letters started to glow. Beneath CONNECT appeared more floating, three-d icons with fractal quality detail: a metal caterpillar connector for hard-wire link, a phone handset and jello-tube for modem, a slowly tumbling satellite for radio, a computer for local mode. When I touched the satellite it grew as if it were speeding toward me from a great distance and then blew up in a shower of sparks.

The sparks swirled and solidified to form a half-sized man of copper plates and brass rivets, who

floated about two feet above the floor of my apartment, sitting lotus-style. Like the icons over his
head, he didn't appear in Melissa's mirror. He wore
a turban, a glittery vest, and bloomers, and held
many strands of gold thread in his fingers. He turned
eyes of emerald and silver filament to look at me
and gave me a mechanical smile, complete with
hinged jaw, lips of rose gold, and teeth of platinum.

"Welcome to Nodality, Inc., a full-spectrum con-
sumer information connect service. Do you wish to
see a list of instructions or options?"

"Thanks, no. Put me through to NewSource."

"As you wish." He sorted his threads, pulled one
loose, and laid it in my outstretched hand. "Have a
nice day!" Then he flung his hand up and vaporized
to star dust.

I touched the gold thread to the floating keyboard
and it wiggled into a port that appeared there. A
new tune played, jazzier than GridLink's, something with trumpets, and a blue planet marbled with
white froth formed over Melissa's bed. The world
had a single moon and a ring of tumbling ice crystals in exotic shapes that caught the sunlight and
wove rainbows. The ice and rainbow braids tumbled
about amid a string of planetoid-sized, hypervisible
crystalline words that circumscribed the planet:

NewSource NewSource NewSource NewSource

The planet grew till it filled the room, swept the
room away with its mass, and then a giant ice *O*
swallowed me. My body vanished and the mote that
was me began to drop toward the planet. The
GridLink menu bar and keyboard went before me at
arm's length, though I had no arms or voice to interface with.

With no body to limit me, my visual range encompassed all directions at once. The horizon below was curved, muted by haze. The sun rose and chased shadow across the ocean. Weather systems whirled lazily across the world's face and electric latticework blazed on the nightward continents. Overhead, the "NewSource" ice rocks trailed backward, barely visible, across indigo sky, gleaming amid faint stars.

A wind rushed past and clouds billowed up, pelting me with snow crystals. Below, toy ships left tiny white wakes in a sapphire ocean that rushed at me. Just before I struck, my vector shifted, and land— desert browns, jewel-white sand, and city neon— flashed by.

It was Los Angeles. I recognized the boulevard lights from jello-flicks, and there was the "Hollywood" sign, and Sky Rail. A glimpse of Phoenix, too, and Las Vegas, then Denver in the Rockies and up through the Grand Tetons to the Canadian wheat fields, then southeast across the dying cities of the Great Dustbowl, and finally I burst into a virtual Chicago and exploded through an open window into the penthouse of the Sears Tower.

Dead silence. A vast foyer surrounded me. Even the silence had echoes. Shiny black floors spread like a pool of oil, and pillars of Martian-red, polished stone held up the improbably distant ceiling. Then the snap of quick footsteps shattered the silence—a woman with glow-specs, a note-screen and stylus, hair pulled back, plain black dress, and a friendly, professional smile appeared from the shadows.

"May I direct you to an information source?"

My hand went to my chest and clanked, metaceramic against metal. With a start I looked down at myself, and then laughed in surprise. Reflexively,

I'd pulled up Golem as my persona. Virtual protection against virtual threats.

I touched the menu bar at the top of my vision and replaced the Golem simile with one of my online personae, Red Barbara: a sun-bronzed, mightily thewed warrior princess in a ruby-encrusted leather harness. My hand went to the hilt of my magic broadsword, Eviscerator, slung at my hip.

My other hand still rested on my chest, and I felt my heart thumping against the flesh of its palm. The female AIde asked in the same intonation if she could help me. I shook my head, waved her away, tried to catch my breath. These newsgrids, sheesh. All I'd wanted was a little e-news.

A CRIMINAL CASE

A familiar voice rasped, "Whither ho, Your Most Excellent Highness?"

I looked down at my sword. The miniature demon face on the knob of the hilt leered at me and tendrils of glowing green ectoplasm trickled up around my wrist from inside the scabbard. Eviscerator couldn't help leering, or rasping. It was hardcoded into his behavioral routines. I patted his head.

"Go to sleep, O Stalwart Companion. No adventures today."

Eviscerator dutifully closed his topaz eyes and the ectoplasm dissipated. Whipping my ponytail back over my shoulder, I looked around. A fabulous variety of creatures—humans and humanoids, animals existing and extinct, machines, creatures unheard of except in myths, things that could not possibly be animate—thundered or strode or fluttered or slithered or staggered in and out among the shadows of the pillars.

Groups gathered here and there, in pockets of shifting outdoor scenery or interior scenes that depixelated into blue-red-green snow about the edges. Toward the center of the building there was a permanent fixture, an outdoor sanctuary. A jungle, judging from the palms, banyan trunks, and viny leaves there. Flashes of bright color—tropical birds— battered the air within the leaf canopy, with cries that sliced the quiet. Among the pillars padded a silent tiger, crossing from blinding sunlight into shadow and back.

The glowing, enamel-on-block signs that hung high up among the pillars matched the selections on my menu bar. Along with various archives, mail exchanges, reinteractments of major news events, and meeting lounges both public and private, was DAILY NEWS DESK.

From the menu bar, I adjusted the simile's reality coefficients. The Sears Tower penthouse imagery receded from hypervividness to something tolerable. As I tinkered with the values my apt appeared, a faint glaze overlaid on the scene. Then I accessed the Daily News Desk from the menu bar, not bothering with the full-reality interact mode that entailed walking over and play-acting with the AIdes and other users' personae. It was more expensive and took longer, and I wasn't here to play today.

When I cued "Nasser" on my *virtu*-keyboard, a matte amber screen appeared before me and strands of dark-green letters spilled across it. Sixteen UPI, AP, Reuters, and Suisse-Nette stories appeared with his name in them somewhere, all but two of them hyperkeyed.

I called up one of the hyperkeyed files—*Police Commissioner Refuses to Release Details of Wealthy Philanthropist's Death*—by touching the headline, which ploded the story onto a new, second screen cast a few centimeters in front of the first.

The police commissioner was quoted as saying that the investigation was ongoing and that they would release an official report in conjunction with the district attorney's office on Friday, once the autopsy was complete. That was today. At least I wouldn't have to wait much longer.

I touched the hyperkey "autopsy," reverse-imaged in silver on a dark-green block, which ploded a sidebar with some unofficial stats from the early forensics reports. Cause of death, massive abdominal hemorrhages. No shit, I thought. Other injuries were amputation of the right arm at the humerus, severe contusions and abrasions on head, the remaining arm, and chest; multiple compound fractures to both legs. I hadn't remembered those.

The secondary hyperkeys ploded 360-degree, slowly rotating holograms of the autopsy that I thought were totally disgusting. I couldn't believe they were publishing them, much less that the police would have released them. They must have been smuggled out, maybe by the same inside source who'd given Corbin my name. I cancelled the sidebar article with its hyperkeys and subscreens, and it imploded back into "autopsy" on the original screen.

Under the "district attorney" hyperkey was a statement by the DA that no decisions had been made but they were "pursuing a joint investigation with an arm of the federal government, looking into possible criminal activities" related to the case.

Who else could they possibly have anything on but me, and what else could it be but the diamonds?

I tried to force myself not to jump to conclusions, to continue reading, but after reading the next sentence over three times without understanding it, I gave it up and dumped all the articles into my beanie's nonvolatile memory. Then I called up the GridLink icons and disconnected.

The Sears Tower penthouse dissolved. I was sweat-soaked, limp-armed, staring with my mouth hanging open at a cola-colored roach waving its antennae about on the underside of my control panel. When I reached up the insect zipped away, squeezing through a crack.

I pushed the panel shelf up, thinking, don't panic, little guy. I've had my fill of crushings for a while.

I chewed a nail for a few minutes, thinking. Whether they were building a criminal case against me or not there was nothing I could do but sit tight. After stripping out of my T-shirt and cutoffs—the apartment was furnace hot—I hid the blink-beanie away again, wiped the sweat out of my eyes, turned on the jellovision for background noise, and got my tools out to work on the air conditioner compressor.

SPIDERS AND TANKS

GOLEM isn't my only waldo. I have Tiger, a minia-ture training tool built like an old World War II tank with two taloned arms, a single IR-to-UV wavelength zoom camera in the turret, and an exceptional sound reception mechanism set in the gun barrel. He fits in the palm of my hand and is totally useless except for scaring the tenement cats or spying on the neighbors (who believe me have nothing happening in their lives worth spying on). And I also have a spider waldo, Rachne; that's Greek for *spider*, I think. Rack-Knees is what Melissa used to call her.

Rachne's older than Golem, even, half deaf and blind, and equally stupid. Fine manipulation's her thing. She weighs about eighty pounds and has ten legs that can also be used as arms, with the right fittings, and can support fairly heavy loads—up to a few hundred kilos, maybe—but she can't haul the bulk Golem can. Which makes her worthless for salvage but, it occurred to me, could make her handy in the recovery and selling of goods.

Once the air conditioner was working again I went down to the cellar. Rachne'd gotten rusty and filthy over the years and was covered with cobwebs. I opened her abdominal cavity and pulled out her hand fittings. Breakage and loss had reduced her original complement of twelve hands to two: a three-fingered Salisbury hand whose synthetic rubber fingertips had grown porous and were falling off, and a crab claw with a tendency to stick half open.

I staggered up the four flights of stairs with Rachne, dodging half-clad filthy kids and cranky housewives, brought the machine inside, and set her up in the middle of the apt floor. After I got her plugged in to get her batteries started recharging, scoured off the rust, oiled all her leg joints real good, and air-cleaned her circuitry, I jacked into my-her linkware and ran operations tests.

The way the apt lurched around I felt like I'd junked on acid. Phosphorous yellows and reds and sea-bottom green dripped down the walls and bled all over the floor. I-Rachne rotated her vidi platform for a look around and collapsed sideways in a twitching jumble. My-her struggles to untangle her legs resulted in mechanical apoplexy. After a few seconds I disengaged, nauseated. I had to unsnarl her legs and wrestle her back upright before I started over.

It's always disorienting to switch machines. But Rachne's linkware hadn't stood the test of time too well, either, and we did not make a good team. I-she kept dropping things, bumping into walls, falling down in a mass of legs. It felt like I was wrestling a bear in corn syrup.

I finally unplugged for a break, wiped the sweat off my face and neck, and then threw the rag over the squatting little beast. She crouched there like a weird suit rack with this stained purple cloth draped over her core and her stick knees poking up all around.

I felt sad, looking at that ancient machine. I missed Golem.

It'd be stupid to go after the diamonds then. Even if Vetch wasn't out there watching me—and he was—the cops might be. Nasser's family would have reported the missing diamonds by now, and after that "criminal investigations" article on the nets I was half-convinced they knew it was me that took them.

But there was no way I could be convicted as long as they didn't find the diamonds and envelope. All I had to do was sit tight and leave the package where it was until things blew over.

But I dreamed on them, though. I jacked back into

Rachne and worked her and watched JV while I tuned the linkware, and oh I dreamed.

COMBAT THE
INFO-JUNK EXPLOSION

NYNET was really pushing JelloNet subscriptions. Some people call JV the poor man's *virtu*, but a subscription to their total interface service isn't at all how they made it sound. The commercials made me laugh.

"Plug into JelloNet," the man in the JV said, *"the latest in jellosystem technology, all the convenience of a* virtu *net, without the cost! Throw those modems, e-mail machines, scanners, facsimiles, and voice answering machines away! For a set of low monthly fees you can plug into NYNET's system and have the convenience of all these at your fingertips, and keep up with all the latest hardware and software advances—automatically!"*

Such a deal. But the NYNET commercial that came on a half hour later was even better. Same actor, different shtick.

"When you log in to collect your jellosystem messages," he said, *"do you find your capture devices overflowing with an endless barrage of electronic ads, promotional gimmicks, merchandise and sales pitches? Try NYNET's Ad-Filter system! A simple selection of keywords will let you filter out the advertising and promotions you don't want, and allow into your system those you do! Nothing could be simpler!"*

Notice: they charge you a monthly fee for gadgets

that collect loads of advertising info-junk, and a fee on top of that to weed the info-junk out. Well, I had a much better method for keeping the info-junk explosion at bay. I ditched all the NYNET rental options and answered the phone myself.

The advertisers figure that the *virtu* nets are the human norm and the jello-nets are for the absolute lowest form of sentient life, so if you have only a basic, video/audio connection to the jellosystem, you're down among the benthic organisms and not worth bothering with.

I didn't even use an answering machine any more, since our old one went the way of the Osborne and the Edsel. If I didn't want phone calls, I didn't answer the phone.

It made life a lot simpler, believe me. Even if I did get tired of being Melissa's pimp.

FACES IN THE JELLY, ONE

"LET me speak to Melissa."

"She's not here right now. Can I take a message?"

"Yeah, tell her William called. I'm free tonight. I'll be at Figuero's at two."

FACES,
TWO

"Is Melissa McDougall there?"

"No, she's not. Can I take a message?"

"I don't know, can you? Ha ha."

Pause. "Look, what do you want?"

"Sorry. I—it's reflex. I'm an English professor. That is, I"—cough—"I'm in town for a few days and my name is John—that is to say, I understand that she—that is, if she's interested in a date—"

"Leave your number and I'll tell her you called."

FACES,
THREE

"I don't want to talk to you again, bitch. Put your roommate on."

"She's not here, Mr. Calen, but we'll have the month's rent to you by next week—"

"You deadbeats owe me five thousand sixty-five fucking dollars for April and this is the last fucking straw. You can fucking tell Melissa if she doesn't have the fucking money for me by Monday you're out on the fucking street, the both of you."

"I'll be sure and tell her, Mr. Calen."

"Fuck you."

Faces,
Four
___

"Put Melissa on."

"She's not here, and she wouldn't want to talk to you if she was."

"Look." Long pause. "I said I was sorry. I paid for the patch work, didn't I?" Another pause. "Look, I know she's there. Stop jerking me around and just put her on."

"Listen, asshole, because I'm only going to say this once. Melissa isn't interested in talking to you any more. If you call again I'm going to send Golem over to bif-bam your head."

"Nobody threatens me!"

"I just did. And I meant it. Blow away."

Faces,
Five
___

"Well, if it isn't Ripoff Ruby."

"Vetch. What a thrill. Is this a social call or did you want to give me a tally on toilet paper squares?"

A smirk. "Something like that. I thought you should know that I've been logging your net time for the last several months in case it proved useful sometime."

That squeezed a gasp out of me. The blink-beanie—it must have had a tracer. I'd used it five or six days a week for the past three months, and for a month-long stretch I'd been on the nets several hours a day. That was more time than it sounded like, too; time passes a lot faster in the nets than outside. So the nets charge by the connect-second.

I pasted on a lip-thin smile. "Nice try, but I scrapped that blink-beanie for parts ages ago."

"Oh, we both know better than that. Two hundred eighty-three connect-hours over the past four months, let's see—that comes to a mega-second, more or less. I believe you've racked up about one hundred and twenty thousand dollars' worth of connect charges. And you know what? I'm going to take it to the police." He laughed. "Don't look so scared. Maybe the nets will just debit your account for the money you've stolen. On the other hand, maybe they'll put you away for ten years."

He had me. I started to tremble. "You're a snake. A *snake.*"

Vetch showed teeth. "I want my money. You owe me fifty-two thousand dollars. You better find a way to pay or you'll be up on e-theft charges."

I Send E-Mail

I spent the next two hours at my vintage, flat-screen, 986 peecy, decrypting the beanie's opsys source code. And I found the tracer: the primary encryptor routine used the ID chip embedded in the helmet to generate false IDs in the connect programs' camouflage routines. Vetch must have had a copy of the encryptor's decryption counterpart, so he could trace the camouflage ID codes and detect when I was on the nets.

Since it was hard-wired in I couldn't simply change the beanie's ID code. And worse, when I removed the chip the helmet's net connect software didn't function. Period.

The urge to throw the whole disassembled mess out the window was overpowering. Not only would that eliminate the evidence; it'd be incredibly satisfying to see the parts crunch and bounce all over the pavement, after all the trouble that stupid device was causing.

Instead I sat there embedded in gel with beanie parts scattered about and thought for a while. And it came to me that the log was a weapon he couldn't afford to use against me unless he was prepared to incriminate himself as well. And Vetch was a bona fide coward. So really, I was safe. As usual he was all noise and no motion.

I put the blink-beanie back together, put it on, and sent some e-mail to one of Vetch's accounts.

All right. You win. Go ahead and turn the logs in. Maybe they'll grant me immunity when I agree to turn state's evidence against _you_ for giving the beanie to me in the first place.

----<Ruby>----

Then, since I was logged into the beanie linkware anyhow, I accessed the Nasser articles again. They were mostly retrospectives and gossip sheets. Nasser, a naturalized American citizen, came from a long line of wealthy Egyptian politicians, and was survived by one wife, second, one son, grown, and assorted more-distant family relations.

Of the tabloid trash, one batch argued back and forth across the newsnets over who'd get the inheritance, which I gathered was stunningly huge, and another batch made bitchy remarks about the wife and son. I didn't spend much time with those, except to note that the will was due to be read on Saturday afternoon. It occurred to me that he was likely to have named the diamonds in his will, and when they turned up missing . . . but that was paranoid. There would be no reason for them to think of me, and the insurance would cover the loss. Unless someone had seen him wearing them, beforehand—?

Well, that was possible. And who else could have taken them but me?

Sit tight, Ruby, I told myself. Even if they suspect you—even if they were certain—they would never find the diamonds where you hid them. How could you be convicted without the evidence? And even if you were convicted, the diamonds would still be there when you got out. All you need to do is just sit tight till the storm passes.

A couple of the tabloid-type articles mentioned me—or rather "Ruth"; those people really knew how to do their homework—and Peter Corbin's account of my account of Nasser's death. One imaginative paranoiac hinted around about who wanted him dead and how much I got paid to do the job. It occurred to me I'd have to be careful with my money for a while, once I'd sold the diamonds, or people might really wonder things like that.

Most of the tabloid contingent were a lot more interested in the money, it seemed, than with the man. That made me feel a little sad for him again.

Some of the retrospectives were better. A number of famous people talked about his accomplishments. He'd sure done an awful lot for a lot of causes. The man had given more money away at a single gesture than I'd see in my lifetime. He'd made a career of charity, touring the world to raise funds for various organizations.

He'd be missed by a lot of people. It amazed me how many famous names I'd heard of knew him. Lots of important people had something to say about him dying, and none were happy about it. And I got to hearing them in my head, the voices of all those people he'd helped, all his admirers. They said how "Ruth" Kubick could have saved his life but tragically failed. Good thing my name's not Ruth, I decided, or I'd get depressed.

WHAT TO WEAR?

A sixth call came in a bit later, while Master Cho and his assistants and I were moving through the slow *kata*, dripping sweat, cooling down. I flicked the reception over to the phone. Given the hour— at almost three-thirty P.M. it was several hours after Manhattan's phase-one workday—it was quite a surprise to see Captain Nano-whatever's face in my tube.

I snatched up a towel, wiped myself down, and, as a defensive measure, tried to summon up nasty thoughts. But I couldn't hold on to the anger. Looking at her face and knowing how easily she could destroy my life made me sick and made my palms cold with sweat. I had a nervous urge to smile but that would have been disastrous; I kept my expression blank.

"Ms. Kubick. Captain Nanopoulos here."

"Captain." I didn't try to say her name. "I didn't expect a call this late."

She gave me a brief smile but didn't offer an apology, so I forged ahead. "Is everything OK with G-Golem?" The stutter really blew my chill act; my face heated up.

I couldn't read her expression, but the pause before she spoke didn't seem too good. "We need to ask you a few questions, Ms. Kubick, and we'd like you to come down to the station."

"I didn't hurt the old man."

"We're not accusing you of hurting him; we simply want to ask you a few questions."

I chewed my lip. "When?"

"Immediately."

My head felt like a balloon someone had poked holes in—I'd walked into a nightmare. A little idiot in the back of my head fussed: what to wear, what to wear.

Do Not Pass Go

Adrenaline fueled me down the stairs at a high speed. I weaved around the adolescents loitering on the second-floor landing and they stared at me, whispered and giggled.

"Hey, Ruby, where's your machine?" one asked, then turned back to the others and said in a stage whisper, "She's so *jade*."

"You going *out*? Look, comrades, sister Ruby's going out. Shee-*euw* are you dressed! You smell like a cologne commercial!"

A burst of laughter swelled up. I ignored them, the little smartasses, and skipped down the last eighteen steps to the ground floor. I hopped over Mr. Gillis, who was out stone-drunk on the first-floor landing again, and checked the mailboxes as I went by. Ours was empty and so were the others. No mail, once again.

I shoved the heavy inner door open and the momentum that had carried me down the stairs propelled me through. Beyond the glass doors of the apt lock, heat waves made ghosts of the afternoon's long shadows. A metal trash can lay in the gutter casting a plume of ripe garbage into the street.

When my hand touched the outer door lock it was like I'd run into an invisible wall. My hand gripped the door handle and turned to stone. Panic boiled up in my throat; I shifted my gaze to my hand, willed my fingers to release their grip on the handle. Nothing. Not a twitch. Somebody inside had staged a mutiny and taken over my body. I wanted to yell for help but felt like an idiot. They'd think I'd gone nuts. I know I sure did.

The impasse broke about ten minutes later, when another tenant came up outside and keyed the lock. When he pushed the outer door open I had to step out of the way and that shattered the paralysis. I escaped through the door into the street before it closed again.

The air was hot, but drier than I'd expected. High bug density, as usual. Flies large and small hovered around the trash. I waved away the gnats that were trying to fly up my nose, slapped mosquitoes off my calves and arms, and pulled my wrap close. A woman with an infant sat on the stoop across the way, and a skinny boy with a big belly sat next to them, languidly bouncing a big, soft, red ball that played a rubber-band bass tune, *boing*, *boing*, when it struck. His belly made me think of the old man's, swollen with blood; I winced.

They were looking at me. It wasn't logical but I had this idea they were ogling me, like there was something wrong with my wrap or my sunscreen face paints that they could see but I couldn't. I felt like yelling at them but I knew that was crazy, so I resisted, and headed for the monorail station.

GIVE ME A GOLEM
AND HOLD THE ROCKS

"YOU wrote a batch demon that deleted your waldo's CASC log every two minutes." The young man looked up from his hand-held kelly through specs perched on the bridge of his nose and raised his eyebrows at me.

He wore a lab coat with a tiny pin on the lapel that said "Associate Commissioner." His china-blue eyes peered through long, thick, auburn eyelashes that Melissa would kill to have. Otherwise he had a plain, pockmarked face and dull red hair amid which nestled a mushroomlike, metallic nub: his beanjack. So he was a beanhead like me—except his no doubt was the latest model. He was also incredibly skinny and tall with hands so strong, long-fingered, and agile *I'd* have killed to have them.

Beside him was the precinct captain, hands in her pockets, watching me with that thoughtful look.

And I had the feeling from the way they kept from getting between me and the big wall mirror that there were people watching from behind there, too.

They'd locked me in the bare room again, with three glastic chairs and a table this time and those same prison windows. Only this time it really was me facing them. Not a happy moment in my life.

Golem's CASC log is a digitized video-audio recording of everything that happens to him and it's restricted-access, only allowed to be touched by Computer and Artificial Systems Commission reps, and only under certain conditions—such as accident investigations. The log is hard-wired against altering and you can't view it without special equipment. It can be deleted if you know the opsys language but it's illegal to do so without archiving the log.

After a while, though, the CASC log burns up so much memory that everybody who knows how to hacks into the system and deletes the log occasionally. Almost nobody bothers to archive the old log in the CASC database—except government-secured AI companies that have to fill out those tedious 62-Qs every quarter. It's no worse a crime than copying a gamer's laser disk, or hitchhiking.

Which, in my current situation, was no great comfort—because if they couldn't get me for murder or theft they'd probably ice me on overblown charges of computer crime. This certainly explained the criminal investigation that the DA's office had mentioned in that article I'd read.

I shoved my hands between my knees, hunched my shoulders in my single good gauze drape—a hooded dress drape in burgundy and tangerine, with my mother's heirloom garnet brooch at the shoulder—looked from him to her, and nodded.

The air was overwarm and dead still and that had to be deliberate. Sweat kept popping out on my face and torso and when it started to roll it felt like tiny flies walking down my skin. Beneath the perfumed powders and deodorants, I stank like fear. The acid in my stomach and intestines threatened; I had a horrible fear I'd lose bowel control and fart.

Nevertheless, by some miraculous contortion of will I managed to hold my voice steady. "I had to. Otherwise the buffer would have interfered with Golem's motor operations."

The man exchanged a look with the captain, and I swallowed spit. I was lying; I hadn't monkeyed with the CASC buffer till after I'd taken the old man's goods, well after we'd made it down off the scaffolding.

"Cel?"

The man shook his head. "We filled several of the unit's auxiliary buffers with data and essentially all of its critical motor operations remained operational."

The captain and the CASC commissioner looked at me again. In for a penny, I thought, and sat forward with a deep breath and a sudden determination. I could out-argue this beanhead.

" 'Auxiliary?' " I repeated. " 'Essentially all?' You couldn't have tested his CASC buffer itself; he's got all the hard-wired controls against it. And the location of the buffer can be as critical as its size in a memory-depleted situation."

Again the captain threw a look at the CASC rep, and again he raised his eyebrows. "Possible, but unlikely. Our tests were thorough."

"I was climbing down a building in a six-point hurricane, for Christ's sake. I couldn't afford the risk!"

"My analysis shows you would have had enough memory without deleting the CASC buffer. It was a clear violation of CASC protocols."

"Well, excuse the hell out of me for putting life and livelihood above your petty bureaucratic protocols!" By this time I was on my feet, trembling, fists clenched. Nothing gets you worked up quicker than a guilty conscience.

The CASC man stepped back, alarm on his face. The captain interposed herself between him and me. Two large males in uniform with stun sticks entered the room and stationed themselves at the door.

"Sit down," the captain told me. She sounded like she meant it.

Ice out, Ruby. I dropped back into the chair, took another deep breath, and met the captain's gaze. "At the time it didn't seem like I had a choice."

The captain looked at me for a moment, then made a "hmph" noise and dismissed the CASC beanhead.

The lieutenant who'd questioned me the first time came in as the beanhead went out and went over to the captain. She and he held a brief, hushed conversation and then he left again.

"If you're going to arrest me I have the right to legal counsel," I said.

The captain nodded. "You do. But as I pointed out before, we're not charging you with anything."

"But you still have to appoint someone, don't you, if I can't afford a lawyer?"

"Like I said, though—" She broke off when the door opened again and the lieutenant held the door for a slim envie woman in her mid-forties.

The envie woman passed me and a scent of musky-sweet spice like incense and tropical flowers trailed her. She wore a lightweight, formal-dress cool suit with gold buttressed epaulets, inset French lazy-C heels, and an ice-toned light pattern. It took main force to tear my gaze away from the bursts, curves, and swirls of light that traced her form.

She extended a bejeweled hand to the captain. Her black and golden hair was sculpted, polymerized in a single standing wave with sparkles, and her face had the texture and color of pale obsidian. Her slick, crimson lips had a slight pout, her nose was narrow, and her green eyes were black-rimmed, Egyptian-style.

When she glanced at me her made-up eyes had a weird look in them, bright and shocky, like nerves and euphorics were the only things keeping her together. The smile she gave the captain had that same plastic quality. But her voice was all melody and smoothness.

"Sheila."

"Rachel. Thanks for coming down. This is Ruby Kubick, the young woman from Queens who tried to rescue your husband. Rachel Karam," she said to me, gesturing at the woman.

The woman turned and looked me up and down. The muscles around her eyes and mouth twitched, and I wondered if she was trying to keep from showing revulsion.

My hands gripped the chair seat.

"My thanks," she said, with an accent that reminded me of the old man's. She must be Egyptian like her late husband.

Her thanking me was too jade; it gave me the creeps. I didn't let anything show on my face, though, merely shrugged. She dabbed her eyes with a lace hanky and turned to the captain. "The funeral home is prepared to receive Youhanna's body. . . ."

"Fine. Lieutenant Rivera will help you with the formalities."

"Will you be able to attend?"

"I'd be honored to." She paused. "Words must be small consolation to you now, but I and many others looked up to him. His loss will be deeply felt."

The woman's face twisted and an awful sound forced its way out of her throat. The captain spoke to her softly and laid a hand on her shoulder. A couple of tears spilled out of her eyes.

Meanwhile the eyes of the two uniformed cops and the lieutenant were boring into the back of my neck. I was starting to feel about the same way a bug must when the cat's attention wanders. Every muscle in my body was strung as tight as piano wire and I wanted to run screaming. Was this some subtle torment; were they trying to get me to lower my guard?

"Have you recovered Youhanna's hypercat yet?" the envie woman asked. The captain nodded.

"We dredged the bay and found the yacht not far from the scraper where Ms. Kubick reports he was stranded. It appears to have capsized in the turbulence, so it checks with Ms. Kubick's story. Lieutenant Rivera will turn over to you all of his personal effects that were recovered from the yacht."

The woman nodded and dabbed her eyes. They had a glimmer in them, a nervous intensity. "What did you find?"

The captain glanced at the lieutenant, who shook his head. "I'll be glad to show you, ma'am. Nothing much. Maps, boating tools, and so on. A change of clothes and some boots."

"That's all?" she asked the lieutenant, over her shoulder. "Nothing else?"

The lieutenant nodded. The woman's glance went to me and her expression flickered. I was suddenly certain: she knew I'd taken the diamonds.

The captain's attention sharpened.

"What's missing?"

The woman shrugged and her gaze slid away from me, back to the captain. "I can't imagine. I didn't board the yacht, only saw him off at the dock that afternoon before he—"

Then she broke off and struggled with tears. This time, though, her struggle felt phony to me, and I think the captain felt the same way. She looked from the woman to me to the woman again, and her eyes had narrowed.

Nanopoulos wasn't the only one who was confused. The only thing I knew for certain was that the envie woman wanted me to have those diamonds. Or she didn't care if I had them. She hadn't reported them missing. And she hadn't mentioned the envelope, either.

I had this sudden, stabbing desire to know what was in that envelope, to hold the diamonds in my hands, to make it all real. A terrible fear filled me that someone had found my cache and stolen the contents. Not a realistic fear given where they were hidden, but I couldn't shake it.

The captain scowled and made some more "hmph" noises while eyeing me and then told the lieutenant to return my waldo to me. The lieutenant took me into the main precinct room and made me sign some forms, and then took me to the storeroom.

JUNKYARD BAIT

THEY'D shoved Golem in a corner among stacks of vivisected computers and electronics equipment. He towered over the gutted electronics, a skeletal giant, inner parts and wires exposed all over, smashed chassis, arms missing, camera eye dangling.

I thought I was prepared for it. But seeing him there like that, it was too much to bear. I burst into tears. The lieutenant, looking embarrassed, handed me a handkerchief. I thanked him, wiped my eyes and nose on my drape, and used the hanky on Golem's chassis instead.

After prying open one of Golem's chest panels I pulled out my waldo beanie. It's similar to the blink-beanie only it doesn't have the decorative row of LCDs and it doesn't connect me with the nets. Its CPU contains a stripped-down version of the waldo linkware. I hate piloting Golem with the beanie but there wasn't any other way to get him home.

I also got out a can of siloxane hydraulic fluid, a hand-case of tools, and some Teflon patch tape from pockets in my baggy pants. When I pulled him out from the wall I got a good look at the Coffin. The dried bloodstains on the FlexBind webbing made me cringe.

I powered him up long enough to check his reserves. The gauge said he'd used up the main power packs and was on emergency reserves now, but that should be enough to get him home. I reached in and dug among the snarl of wires and tubes of Golem's innards, feeling for the main hydraulic lines.

"What are you doing?"

I sat back on my knees, wiped the slickness from my fingers, and favored him with a look. "What does it look like?"

"You can't do that here, lady. Fix him at home."

"Look. He's not going to get ten feet without I patch his worst hydraulic leaks. Do you want him out of here or not?"

He frowned at me.

"Maybe we should get Captain Nanopoulos to settle this," I added.

"Just hurry up about it," he said. He lit up a cannabette and smoked it, leaning against the doorjamb, watching me work, which did things to my nerves and made it all take twice as long.

RUBY-ME

ONCE done, I pulled out Golem's FlexBind web and shook it out. "Give me a hand here, would you?"

The lieutenant gave me a *"who, me?"* look.

"Yes, you," I said. "Hold this net, just like this."

He took hold, looking dubious, and I struggled in. I stuffed earplugs in my ears and then put the waldo control beanie on. While the program loaded, I reached up and put a hand on Golem's chassis. "Let's go home."

Then the linkware pulled me into Golem, and somewhere far away I felt my hand fall as if I'd dozed off. I-Golem looked down at the woman in my arms. It was Ruby-me, of course, and her-my eyes were closed, fluttering a little. She-I curled with her-my cheek against Golem's chassis.

She-I looked so young and vulnerable from the outside, not ugly and scrawny like me. I was terrified that I wouldn't be able to keep her from harm; I wished she were back home, safe, right this very minute.

I hate that damn beanie.

It Was Him

It was him, perched on the stoop dripping sweat on the concrete and blocking Golem's and my access. When he saw us coming, he stood up and pulled his silver reflective cape about himself. I somehow wasn't surprised to see him.

"I've been waiting for you to show up," Vetch said.

"What now?" I put as much disgust as I could muster into Golem's loudspeaker broadcast.

Vetch tossed a data lozenge into the air, caught it, tossed it again. Irritatingly, he stared down at Ruby-me instead of into my-Golem's cameras so I-Golem had a perfect view of his incipient bald spot. "I thought I'd give you one last chance to pay me at least a portion of what you owe me before I go to the police with this evidence of your illegal use of the nets."

I-Golem dragged forward in a whine and clatter of misaligned parts. "We both know you can't report me without incriminating yourself."

"I found the encryption code when you let me borrow the beanie and felt so guilty about it for so long I finally decided to come clean." He spread his hands with a wide smile. "Your word against mine. Who do you figure they'll believe, the crook or the upstanding citizen who turned her in?"

"What is it with you? Don't you know when to quit? I haven't got fifty thousand dollars. I've got nothing to give you. I'm sorry about the data but there was nothing I could do. Leave me alone, already!"

"Prove it. Prove you're sorry."

"How?"

"I'll leave you alone about the fifty-two kay you lost me, if you give me something."

"Like what?"

"Like a portion. Ten thousand."

My heart lurched—my eyes came open and met his. "I haven't got that kind of money!"

He grabbed my gauze wrap through the FlexBind and stuck his face in mine. "Then you better find it. Or this"—he held up the lozenge—"goes to the police. We'll see whose story they believe."

I-Golem grabbed for the lozenge with the telescoper, but Golem was in no condition for a test of reflexes. Vetch danced out of the way, laughing. "Start watching your front door, Kubick. They'll be busting it down anytime now."

Talk about should-have-dones. I didn't even think of bif-bamming him with Golem's schwarzenegger until he was long gone around the corner.

SHE LOVES ME NOT

MELISSA asked, "Rube? That you?"

"Yeah, it's me."

I-Golem clanked and dripped into the entryway, and shut and bolted the door. After parking in the corner between the hall closet and the bathroom door I shut Golem down, pulled the beanie and earplugs off, and scrambled out of the FlexBind. I'd have to put Golem in his usual spot in the cellar in a bit, and clean off those bloodstains, but at the moment I was too tired and irritated to bother.

I pulled my gauze drape off over my head, fluffed my hair out, licked salty sweat from my lips, and sank against the doorjamb with a deep breath. Home, safe.

In the main room, Melissa sprawled over her bed in cutoffs and a choker of plastic pearls and nothing else. She was reading a skiffy zipper-ripper novel, twirling a lock of wet hair with her finger and thumping the bed with her leg. She'd scrubbed off all the layers of sparkle and makeup; her skin was so clean it shone.

"Hey," I said. "I got Golem back."

"Yeah, well, you left all your shit out."

I looked around and realized Rachne and my tools weren't out anymore. I stiffened.

"What'd you do with my things?"

"I dumped them in the cellar. I could barely walk in here."

"Melissa, those are delicate tools and I had them

carefully organized—on *my* bed. You may have ruined them and I need them to fix Golem."

She shrugged a single shoulder. "So don't leave them lying around. Besides, they weren't all on your bed. You left half of them on the floor."

I went down the back staircase to the cellar. Rachne looked OK, over in the corner of my nook, but the tools were another matter. Melissa had thrown them haphazardly into the bottom of my tool cabinet and hadn't even bothered to lock it. When I slid the door back and saw them my hands started to shake. I took the tools upstairs, spread them out on my own bed, and inspected them closely, one by one. By some miracle all of them had survived her careless handling intact.

I sensed she was looking at me and glanced up. I was right. When she met my eyes she burst into laughter.

"They're just a bunch of tools and things. I didn't hurt them. Stop looking so persecuted."

After a moment I said, "Don't ever touch my tools."

She started reading her book again. I wanted to yank her hair and pound on her clean-scrubbed face. Instead I said very quietly, "I mean it. Never touch them."

"OK, I'm sorry." She gave me one of her phony smiles. Sure you are, I thought.

After a minute she asked, "Did I get any phone calls?"

I didn't answer. She raised her eyebrows at me, but I didn't feel like backing down. Not after she messed with my things.

"Rube."

"What?"

"Stop being cute and tell me who called."

I shook my head. "I refuse to pimp for you anymore."

She went pale and sat up. Then her skin flushed red from the breasts up.

"I'm tired of setting dates for you and lying for you and chasing off the shitheads," I went on. "Get an answering machine."

She was silent a full minute, it seemed like, just looking at me. I began to regret what I'd said. She leaned forward and covered her mouth, then straightened. Seeing the look in her eyes, I started to feel sick to my stomach.

She said, "You just pushed me too far."

I didn't say anything.

"How *dare* you call me a whore?"

I didn't call you a whore, Liss. I love you. Let's not fight. Say it, Ruby. But I was tired of backing down to keep the peace.

"They pay you," I said, "and you fuck them. Call it what you want."

She shook her head like she couldn't believe her ears. "At least I've got friends, I've got a life! You spend all your time junked out on your stupid machines. It makes me sick to see you lying there, twitching and drooling and talking to yourself all the time.

"You never get out, you don't have any friends, you expect me to be *everything* to you."

Bif bam. That hurt. She wasn't saying it but I knew she was thinking about the time that asshole sliced up her face. I'd taken her to the hospital, waited those long hours with her in the waiting room, stayed while they patched her up, and helped her home.

She had unplugged from reality; she just sat all afternoon staring out the window and looking fragile, her face and neck covered with oily skinseal patches and bruises. But I held her hand and told her how beautiful she was and how much I loved her, how sorry I was that someone had hurt her, and finally she started to cry. She sobbed and sobbed over the hurt and fear and violence.

Finally she took me to bed and asked me to hold her, and it became more than that. Maybe I should have said no when she kissed me. But I didn't.

If making love is a craft, Melissa is an artisan. Even drugged and hurting the way she was, she put all of her mind and soul right out there, at the surface of her skin. And with her touch, in the places of me where her lips and fingers lingered, she transferred that beauty to me. The touch and smell of her, the arch of her back, her eyes half-slitted, the smile that spread across her lips afterwards, when she nestled in the crook of my arm . . . I watched her sleep, understanding then why all those men always called her back.

In the morning she'd gotten up first and fixed me breakfast, but she didn't want to talk about what had happened; she acted like everything was normal. I sure didn't feel like things were normal.

After a couple of days I'd screwed up my courage and brought up what had happened. She'd said that it'd happened because she'd needed someone to hold her and make her feel sexy, but that wasn't how she felt about me. She sure was convincing the other night, I'd said, but I never mentioned it again after that. The memory of it had stayed with me, though, and it was about as welcome as a sore tooth.

Several times I tried telling my body to stop lusting for her. It had a mind of its own, though, and that's a fact. So what she said stung more than she probably meant it to.

"I never asked you to be anything for me," I said.

"Bullshit. You're always making demands."

"Like what? Name one thing I've asked you to do for me since I came here. One thing."

But she wasn't listening. "I'm tired of you using me. I'm tired of being your crutch."

"My crutch? *I'm* using *you?*"

"Jesus Christ, I spend half my money on groceries to feed you because you won't go outside the apt!"

I frowned. "That's not true. I buy groceries. I sent Golem to the store just last week."

"I buy most of the food and you know it. Besides, it's sick how you never go out. I nearly died from shock when I came home today and you weren't here. That's the first time you've gone out in months." She pressed her hands to her lips again and when she lowered them and looked at me, her face had gone as smooth as a pane of glass.

"I've been wanting to say this for a long time. The truth is that you're really fucked up and you should see someone. Get professional help. Go to the mental health clinic."

I stared at her, flabbergasted. "*I* need professional help? Me? You're the one who'll bed anything with two legs and a penis and ask for spending money. You call those men friends? You call the man who sliced your face open last month a *friend?*

"You stay away for days and then come back and expect the apartment to be spotless, exactly how you left it. You spend most of your time ignoring me except when you can find something to bitch about." *When was the last time you paid your share of the rent?* But those words stalled at my lips.

She'd use that money, all right, if I told her she had to, and then she'd be right back out there, fucking sickos and maniacs to bring in more. No. But I was still trembling with anger. "How can you accuse *me* of using *you*?"

She just stared at me. Then she gave me the finger, grabbed her gauze wrap, and slammed the door on the way out.

I marched Golem down to the cellar and then went to bed. I was exhausted and fell right to sleep. But a bad dream, about how the old man had died, woke me up again around ten-thirty. I got up and roamed the apartment like a caged cat. Four hours wasn't enough sleep but there was no way I could doze off again. I couldn't get Melissa off my mind.

I tried watching jellovision, but nothing good was on and I was restless. And I wasn't about to use that damn blink-beanie and give Vetch more ammunition. There were other things I could do, though. Golem needed replacement parts. The diamonds and the mysterious envelope kept resurfacing in my thoughts. So I geared Rachne up; I figured I had plenty to do to take my mind off Melissa.

I Buy Junk

THE Lone Star Used Parts Yard and Scramport Shuttle Service looked weird beneath the harsh bar-lights of sodium and mercury. Otherwise the place hadn't changed much since the last time I'd been there. The guard cats set up a fearful noise when I-Rachne tripped up to the fence, and a familiar voice yelled, "Who's that? Who's out there?"

I-Rachne tilted her vidi platform up. Lit by the glare of the yard lights, Mikey was squinting down at me from his office on the second story. One hand gripped the short, stout barrel of a semishot, which was aimed in my-Rachne's general direction, and I didn't have to think hard to figure out where the other hand was.

He and everything else was in black, white, and greys; I'd been unable to fix Rachne's color malfunction and had left it turned off. In my head, Rachne's radio transmitter crackled across the sounds of distant traffic and lapping waves like a geiger counter in a nuke dump. So I had this sense I'd been transported into a bad copy of an old flattie. I tweaked her linkware, trying—unsuccessfully—to improve sound reception, then crabbed forward on her stick legs and cranked her volume up.

"It's me," I-Rachne yelled. "Ruby Kubick. Need some parts."

"Ruby, hey! That really you?—Shut up, Pete, Ginger! Cut the caterwauling! Down in a nick."

His head disappeared inside the window. While I waited, I-Rachne did a slow turn, which is a complicated maneuver with her ten legs all clicking and mincing around each other, for the practice . . . and also just to make sure no one—like maybe Vetch or the cops—was sneaking up behind. I-Rachne had sneaked out down the fire escape in the back of the building, and had been very careful getting here, but you can never be too sure.

The only things stirring in the street and the puny dirt parking lot were bits of trash tumbling before the wind—it was a little early for the evening crowds, and not the kind of place where you'd expect to find the dayfolk. Behind the chain-link and barbed-wire fence, piles of metal and rusting machinery filled the yard. Mikey had expanded his in-

ventories since the last time I visited. To the far
right were his two antique helicopters.

Two enormous genie guard cats crouched on the
opposite side of the fence, staring at me-Rachne.
They'd stopped yowling when Mikey'd told them
to, but they were still stiff with hostility—hissing,
muscles bunched, eyes dilated to the whites, ears
laid back. I made a face—a satisfying gesture of de-
fiance, even if they couldn't see it.

A storm was moving in. On the far side of the
yard a row of dead elms clawed the sky. Lightning
laced a dark, boiling thunderhead beyond the row
of ramshackle buildings across the canal and backlit Mikey's silhouette as he descended the stairs.
Through Rachne's eyes the lightning looked like an
X-ray of the storm's skeleton. Mikey still had the
gun, which was only good sense. What with
Rachne's low-res vidis and the poor lighting, I
couldn't make out his face.

" 'Bout time you dropped by! Saw you on the news
the other night and wondered how you been."

Hearing his voice made me grin; I could feel the
tug in my cheek muscles back home. "Hey ya,
Mikey."

"People been asking whether you off and got
yourself indentured to the platforms."

"I wish!"

"This the same model I recall you fixed up away
back when?" he asked, gesturing at me-Rachne.

The linkware automatically translated my nod,
overamplified, and lost its frame of reference. It took
an irritating several seconds thereafter for me to find
Mikey again, and by that time he was close enough
for me to make out his face. He was grinning at me
through the chain link with—as usual—a toothpick
between his teeth. He had scars on his neck and

forehead, a gauze robe on, and his brown hair was all curly and rumpled.

Mikey had been indentured by the Army ten years ago and had spent four years flying collocopters in Antarctica, before the bombs had made that particular piece of real estate too radioactive to fight over. Then the Army had made him obsolete the same way Toshiba-Merrill had me, but all he had to show for it was the scars. That was because when they'd asked me if I wanted the brain web out, I'd said no— I figured outmoded equipment was better than none. But maybe Mikey had the right idea. He made a lot steadier living out of junk than I did.

From the blanket creases on his cheek I'd probably waked him. But this was a twenty-four-hour yard and he must be used to it; his customers were mostly refugees and fringers, who didn't have envie suits or waldos and did most of their outdoors business between midnight and eight A.M.

"She ain't improved much over time," he asked, "has she?"

Indignant protests filled my mouth but I shoved them back down before they could get out. He was right.

"Nah," I-Rachne admitted with a sigh. "I haven't piloted her since I built Golem. Speaking of which, I need parts. Lots of parts."

"Ah." His eyebrows shot up. "Golem must have gotten a trifle more banged up than you let on in that interview."

"Oh." I hesitated. "I didn't want to discourage potential customers."

"Well, hell. I'm surprised they're not beating your door down by now. You're a real hero."

"I sounded like a drooling maroon."

"Not so. You were great."

I could feel my face heating up. "All right, already."

"I mean it. You done good. Hell, *I* was impressed."

"Mikey, shut up."

He grinned at me but let it go. "Where's your wish list?"

"Wait a sec." I put Rachne on standby for a second and, back at the apt, propped myself up on an elbow and checked the sheet of paper in my lap. Then I lay back in the gel and downloaded back into Rachne.

"Got any Pratt and Whitney Series S-Jiminy 40L parts in stock, or any 42Ns? Or GM&E 77-12s?"

"Hmmm. Don't know for sure, but I don't think so. Let's check anyhow, though. They ain't manufactured those in a long time. But I haven't been back there in a while and don't recollect too well what-all I've got."

"And I particularly need some gigacrystals. UAI 8200s. Though I could do with 8100s if I had to."

He got a thoughtful look on his face. "Yeah? UAI 8200s?"

"You got some?"

His expression seemed pained. "Not to sell. They're in Monster Mash."

"Ah." Disappointment settled in my stomach. Couldn't blame him, though. His collocopter Monster Mash was his baby the same way Golem was mine. And I wouldn't gut Golem for parts no matter how hungry I got.

He gnawed on his toothpick with an earnest expression. "What else?"

"Tubing, metaceramic plate, structural titanium. Assorted odds and ends. Let's see what you've got."

He unlocked the gate and opened it. I-Rachne

danced inside with her interlocking gait, and rotated the vidi platform to keep an eye on those guard cats. I didn't care how gene-mod clever and obedient they were: the last thing I needed was damage to another one of my units.

Mikey walked me-Rachne past his helicopters on the way to the waldo stockpiles, which was a little out of the way, and he kept looking at me-Rachne out of the corner of his eye. There was his tiny 1960s bubble-glass model, Tinkerbell, which was the one he'd flown down the street the other night, and looming over it was Monster Mash.

Mash was a turn-of-the-century military bird, a big ugly green thing with sets of two propellers and white stars painted on it and a tail section riddled with holes. He'd been adding equipment, disassembling it, tinkering with it, testing it, and reassembling it for over a year now. As far as I knew he had yet to get it airborne.

I realized why the detour when I noticed he also had one I hadn't seen before, a sleek, aerodynamic black collocopter with five props overhead, tinted windows that made it look like a sky cadillac, and "WAPL News at 11" painted in luminous letters on the sides that looked silvery through Rachne's eyes. I broke into a smile and I-Rachne pointed with her rubber-coated talon. "New one?"

"Yup."

"You named it yet?"

He grinned and spat out his toothpick, which was a splintered, mushy mass of pulp by now. "Not yet. Got it at a discount when the station that owned it went belly up. I've flown it once. On manual, of course," he said at my surprised look. "With specs and gloves. She's a fuel gobbler but she's real fast. Flies lighter'n a piece of dandelion fluff, too."

"Mikey, you have the soul of a poet."

"She's stealthy, too—radar invisible and sonar soft . . ."

"Figures." I laughed. "I bet that's why they went bankrupt. One too many invasion-of-privacy lawsuits."

He laughed, too, open-mouthed barks of sheer hilarity. "Damn straight. And she's a beauty, Ruby. Come on by sometime; I'll take you up and give you a tour of the island you'll be talking about twenty years hence."

I-Rachne made a choking sound. "Thanks, I'd rather die."

He pulled out a new toothpick to maul. He showed me to the various spots and waited while I-Rachne rummaged through his stacks and shelves of metal and plastic waldo remains. I-Rachne found a new headlight and a camera I could use to replace the eye Golem lost. Then I made a real find: two robotic arms that I was sure I could figure out a way to attach and program.

One arm was a newer version of the two finger-handed arms I'd lost: an eight-mutually-opposable-fingered hand on a socket-jointed arm. Both the arm and the fingers had an extra joint. The extra joints and length, and the extra movement of each joint, would take some practice to use but would end up being a real bonus.

The other I was even more excited about. It was true vintage tech, a stroke of great luck: an antique warrior arm—a two-meter snake in a titanium weave sheath, in excellent condition. Its connector was a sister technology to Golem's arm platform. The warrior waldos that'd used snakes had been famous during the Antarctic Conflict for wreaking havoc among enemy equipment. My guess was this particular arm had been manufactured near the end of the Conflict and then never used; it was that clean and unmarked.

The snake had several titanium and metadiamond "hand" attachments for drilling and cutting through metal, and various splicing tools. Six electronic jimmy-jacks, hard-wired into the arm, must have been used for breaking into or interfering with enemy equipment and communications in various ways.

What war waldos use against enemy troops, I could put to good use in salvage—against inanimate obstructions, old electronic locks, security systems, robots, and the like. The arm came with a training and reference chip that could be installed in Golem's crystal. Trey schick.

I-Rachne found several other useful odds and ends. But the most crucial items, memory gigacrystals, he didn't have. Looked like I would be seeing the insides of a lot of junkyards and two-hand stores over the next few weeks. I-Rachne cast a last, covetous look at Monster Mash as we passed the copter on our way toward the front of the yard.

Mikey tallied up the cost on his hand-held kelly. After wrapping the purchases, I-Rachne dropped them in the carriage sack beneath Rachne's belly. Rather than tackle his metal stairs in Rachne, I put her on standby again while I disengaged to use our jellophone and transfer the money to his account.

The account balance at the base of the jello-tube was dismally low. With a wince, I hit the transfer button.

"Do you wish another transaction?" the bank's digital ghost-lips asked. I disconnected instead of answering and then sank back into the couch, plugged in, and reengaged with the linkware. Mikey was still chewing his toothpick and eyeing me-Rachne thoughtfully, but I couldn't tell what he was thinking.

"You change your mind about the UAI 8200s?"

He shook his head with a sympathetic laugh. "Sorry, Ruby. I may be a mercenary fucker, but I don't sell family."

"Just checking," I-Rachne said. "I'll wait while you verify the transfer."

Mikey laughed and waved a hand.

"You I trust," he said. "You're straight."

That gave me a queer little flutter in the stomach, remembering the dead old man's bare ears.

"Thanks, Mikey."

"Come by again," he said. "Next time come in the morningtime when Amity spells me, and bring yourself along like the old days, instead of this old bucket of bolts. Some of the guys been asking about you. We'll stand you breakfast."

"Sure. It'd be a lot of fun."

I could tell by the look in his eyes, though, that he figured I wouldn't, and I didn't get out much anymore so I figured he was probably right.

WE DO THE CITY

AFTER that I-Rachne spent hours wandering the streets of Soho and the Village. Early on, the storm struck; umbrellas bloomed like a field of canvas wildflowers. I didn't trust Rachne's construction well enough to stay out in the wet—she's strictly a DO NOT IMMERSE machine. So I-she stood in the doorway of a boutique till the storm passed, and the spread of umbrellas furled and died.

Then I-she went back out and lingered in front of shops and delis and art galleries, restaurants and slidewalk cafés and theaters, tripping over her too-many feet and drawing an occasional rude stare from the tourists and locals crowding the walkways and streets in their cool suits, waldos, and wraps.

The street traffic rushed past—electric collocars and -buses, motorcyclones, handcarts, pedal carts, rickies, and bicycles—and the canal traffic floated in the middle of the avenue: the flopeds and globe-lit, tourist-filled gondolas that rocked in the wakes of speedboats, pixiboats, and the sleek hypercats that skimmed the surface of the water like dragon-flies.

I-she passed a dock filled with plain little row-boats with strings of ugly bare bulbs made beautiful by simple reflection and repetition. Wind, music, sirens, horns, voices, machines—the sounds swirled around each other, merged and collided like ocean waves against a barrier reef. Rachne, like Golem, has no olfactory or tactile temperature sense, but I could almost smell the bitter-fresh ozone, feel the wind on my face.

It'd been so long since I'd been on the streets, I'd forgotten what an elixir the city is—faces and masks and paint, legs and arms, suits, wraps, and mostly naked bodies—lights on water, angles and manne-quins and machines and humanity, electric flashes, steam and running water from holes and grates—all these impressions and glimpses flowed around me; even in black and white it captured me, made me love it again.

The city distills life into some intoxicant, an en-ergy more dangerous than any designed drug, that flows through the streets and binds you up in it, if you let it. If Melissa could have heard me thinking that, she'd have laughed. But she's caught by it, too. And I suppose it's easier to love such a place when your awareness is encapsulated in a metal body that puts nothing of you at risk. So I-Rachne wandered and sipped at the streets of Manhattan from my safe haven in Queens.

Till very, very late. Till I was sure that no one could possibly be following me.

THE STASH

THE notorious brownstone at 178 Christopher Street, where the terrorists who blasted the Antarctic ice shelf loose built their atomic bombs, is still standing after all these years and is still hot.

The row of buildings is cordoned off from Bailey House at Weehawken to the burned-out apartment complex at Washington Street. To keep the sea and other trespassers out, the street's blocked off with a thirty-foot concrete dike and topped with concertina wire. Big signs in yellow and maroon warn people off and the area around it has gradually been abandoned. Everyone keeps away. So getting over the fence unnoticed was easy.

I-Rachne jumped from the edge of the dike and alighted with a clatter of metal feet on the street inside the barricade. Nothing had changed in three days. Lights on Washington and Weehawken carried faintly. Paper and dead rats littered the street. A knocked-over fire hydrant dangled from an eight-inch pipe around chunks of sidewalk. The windows were mostly shattered; doors leaned open. Beyond the dike, in the distance, traffic rushed past and a ship's horn blew.

I-Golem had tested the area earlier. 178 Christopher had plutonium contamination all over the place. So, though Rachne didn't have a geiger counter, I knew radioactivity levels were significantly elevated even where I-Rachne stood over a block away. Even machines can be hurt by radiation; to avoid damage to Golem's circuitry and keep from radioactivating his metallics, I'd picked an apartment building closer to the dike.

I-Rachne picked my-her way through the trash, rocks, and dead rodents to 161 Christopher. Scrambling over the rubble that filled the doorway, I-she stumbled but kept her balance. Miraculous. I-she dug the flashlight out of the carriage sack beneath her belly; inside the building it was pitch black, and Rachne has neither lights nor IR vision.

A big crack in the wall, when the flashlight's beam first struck it, brought back the memory from the other time. My heart started to beat like hammer blows. Glimpses of the peeling paint on my own ceiling and the control panel circuitry above my head punctuated my view of the trashed old building. Concentrate, Ruby. This is no time to stutter.

I-Rachne found my-her way to a bathroom in a second-floor apt, and opened the medicine cabinet. The gelpaper packet was still there and so were the diamonds, wrapped in netting and teflon sealant tape.

My mouth went dry and I could feel myself trembling. I-Rachne snatched the bundle up, rolled it into a tight cylinder, and crammed it into the carriage compartment inside her steel-blue belly. Then I-she made for home. I must have tripped poor Rachne up five times in the first twenty feet alone.

RACHNE PLAYS
HIDE AND SEEK

ONE thing about Rachne, she handles stairs better than Golem. I-she debarked the monorail car, passed through the fare turnstile, and clattered noisily down the stairs with the other people and waldos getting off.

Beneath the wrought-iron stairway that leads down, down, down, from the monorail station to street level is a fenced-in lot next to an abandoned building. The chain-link fence has a gash in it peeled back far enough for a child, or Rachne, to get through. I-she lingered until the others at the station had wandered away down Flushing, then slipped through the gap and down into the basement of the nearby building.

I-she dug the flashlight back out and passed through a cluttered, wet underground passage to the next building over. The lock was an old nonmag metal-key type.

Rachne didn't have the software to handle that kind of lock, but I did: the old-fashioned kind. My dad had been a salvage man, too, in a manner of speaking, and I'd picked up a few of his skills as a girl. That was before I'd run away from home at sixteen to join Toshiba-Merrill's waldo mining project on the moon. T-M hadn't treated me much better than my parents had, but the health care was a hell of a lot better and the food more edible than Mom's.

In the loading dock behind that second building, I-Rachne skittered across the yard among the oil stains, dark granular piles, and bulldozers, and then leapt up and caught hold of the wood fence with her legs crooked. Her belly is curved and there was nothing to grip to stabilize her balance; I-she teetered with all ten legs scrabbling against the wood and then fell in a heap into the back alley on the far side. As usual, it took several noisy attempts to stand.

The fire escape ladder up to my apartment was less than two meters away. As I-she started for it, something human-sized moved in my-her periphery. I-she began to turn but her legs folded up like a dropped black widow's and visuals turned to snow. All inputs went dead.

My eyes came open: the control lights on the panel showed red. Someone had snatched her from my control. And there was no lock on her compartment where the diamonds and envelope were.

I yanked the lead, grabbed my keys, and headed down the hall at a dead run. Vetch. It had to be Vetch. Please God please, don't let it be the police.

By the time I reached the fire escape only seconds had passed but there was no movement below. No cops, no police vehicles.

No one could have found out about the diamonds. I'd been too careful. It had to be that she'd been scavenged for parts, by Vetch or someone equally desperate. Nobody else would bother with junk bait like her.

Could I have been followed all that time, without knowing?

I stopped back at the apt only long enough to pull on a pair of cutoffs, grab my tool kit, and yank a wrap and the waldo beanie off the wrap stand. I scooped a big gob of sunscreen from the jar in the bathroom and dashed down the front stairs, smearing the goo on my face, collarbone, and arms. It stung my eyes and made my nose run. The beanie I slung over my shoulder by its chin strap and threw the wrap over it, to keep it hidden.

I built up as much speed as I could going down the stairs so as not to get stuck at the outer door again. It didn't help. I still stalled when my hand touched the grip and an invisible hand closed on my throat so I couldn't breathe. My heart started to race.

Rachne's out there, I told myself. It didn't help. My hand kept its death grip on the handle. I fought so hard my arm began to tremble. Mingled tears and sweat dripped down my face. And the diamonds—they're my one chance to change things. I can change things if I get out there—*now*—but nobody else can do it. This once. Please.

And slowly, slowly, the death grip eased—just enough for me to pull the door open, and bull my way out past the paralysis.

A moldering steam bath of smells, insects, and noise greeted me. Several people were out in the street. The sky was dark beyond the buildings. Wasps and flies hovered and a yellow jacket strafed me. A fair number of bicycles, handcarts, and powered scooters crisscrossed my path, ringing bells and honking. An old, whiskered white man with a spine shaped like a squashed question mark walked slowly by across the street.

I dodged traffic over to him. He flinched when I raised my hand to flag him.

"Excuse me," I said, "did you see someone carrying a spider waldo just now?"

He shook his head.

"A big bag, maybe? Somebody running?"

His eyes glittered at me and his tongue moved in his mouth like a big, wet slug till I could have screamed from impatience. Slowly he lifted an arthritic finger and pointed it toward the monorail. "Tha way."

I flung a thanks over my shoulder and bolted.

It made sense. Whoever had grabbed her wouldn't get far on foot lugging an eighty-pound spider in this heat, and nobody who could afford to own a vehicle would go after Rachne. And if it was Vetch, his warehouse was two stops up the line.

They couldn't know about the diamonds. I'd told no one and I'd hidden them before anyone else had known the old man was dead.

While I was still half a block from the monorail, up high between the lights on the buildings toward Manhattan, a train dropped a curtain of sparks as it braked for the station. I'd never make it.

Then I thought of Rachne and the hidden package. Like hell I wouldn't. I burst into a sprint.

Lungs on fire, grey fingers of blindness in my eyes from too much heat and not enough air, I reached the steps as the train screeched to a halt overhead, and leapt the stairs two and three at a time. The chimes sounded as I stumbled up onto the platform and waved my mag-card at the toll reader.

I hurled myself through the turnstile and toward the train—squeezed through the doors as they slid closed, bashing my tool kit and shoulder. Face hot, pain shooting down my arm, I sagged against a handhold, wheezing, as the train accelerated.

Once I'd recovered some of my wind and my vi-

sion recovered I adjusted my wrap and shrugged my
beanie up onto my shoulder. As my adrenaline levels dropped, the air conditioning made me shiver
and I was so sick to my stomach I didn't know if I
could keep from throwing up. I dropped into a seat.
Breathe slowly, through your nose, my mom'd say.
I did, and it helped.

Once I caught my breath I looked around. The
few other passengers in the car hid behind net specs
or their Sony Bookmans, or burrowed into their
polyback newspapers and books, and paid me no attention. No one was carrying a spider waldo or a
suspicious, large bag.

I'd boarded the third car, which meant there were
two cars behind mine and seven ahead. The back
two first, then, and check outside at each stop. So I
got up and opened the door, and stepped into a blast
of heat and sound: the connector between the car
I'd boarded and the next car toward the back. All
dozen or so passengers were visible through the glass
window. No spider waldo, no bag.

I opened the door, stumbled into the chilly air of
the car and down its length, accelerating by bounds
like an astronaut on the moon as the train deceler-
ated. I yanked that car's door open, got hit in the
face by more heat and noise, and peered through the
glass into the last car of the train.

One of the several passengers was a kid the size
and shape of a boxcar, dark-skinned—possibly
American Indian or Polynesian—dressed in a neon-
splash loin wrap, with studs in his nose, no hair,
and a big, green canvas bag with metallic Rachne
legs sticking out. In spite of his size he looked very
young. Also scared. I ducked back out of his sight.

By this time the train had squealed to a halt. The
kid stayed seated till the bells chimed, then heaved

the bag up and ducked out the door as it slammed shut. The sneak. The train started to inch forward, but I didn't dare jump off till the last second, or for sure he'd see me.

So I ducked between one of the guard chains and the accordion fence and leaned out with a foot on a lower chain, hanging from a shoulder-high handhold. The train sped up to walk-speed, faster, to a run, faster—I leapt up and out and struck the platform hard, barely a meter from the far end. The tool kit slipped from my grasp as I tucked to protect the beanie, and made a terrible clatter on the concrete.

At the far end of the platform, the kid's head was disappearing down the stairs below the level of the platform floor. I couldn't tell whether he'd seen me when he heard the noise or not, but he didn't seem to be moving any faster than before. Maybe he just thought I was a major klutz. If so, he wasn't the only one. As I stooped to pick up the tool kit an oldish woman carrying packages gave me a strange look. She must have seen me jump from between the cars.

I smiled. "I just hate missing my stop, don't you?"

She gave me a nod, a rather vague smile, lots of space, and a surreptitious backward glance.

I snatched up the tool kit and headed for the back end of the platform. From above I spotted the kid. He headed down a side street, looking nervously over his shoulder, and I hurried through the turnstile and down the stairs.

By the time I fell in a short block behind him, he seemed more relaxed. He had lugged Rachne up onto his back and stopped glancing back so much. He turned left onto Metropolitan Avenue, where people crowded the sidewalks and threaded across streets amid the electric-, combustion-, and pedal-powered traffic that crept and surged down the twelve-lane avenue.

I closed in on him. One of the times he looked back he stared right at me, but I closed my face like a commuter in a rush and gave him a *what are you staring at, creep?* look. He glanced away with no expression of recognition or alarm.

And a few blocks later I realized that, just like I thought, he was heading toward Vetch's warehouse.

WE PLAY TAG TEAM

VETCH and the kid were talking below, a sheer, two-story drop from where I sat, straddling the window latch. The kid had entered Vetch's warehouse a moment earlier and I'd noticed some stairs outside the three-story building that went up to a locked door on the second floor.

I'd climbed the stairs, spotted an open window just beyond the railing at the end of the landing, and swung over to the window. Now I sat on the sill, legs dangling, and watched the transaction.

Vetch peeled several bills off a roll and handed them to the kid, who handed over the bag.

"Any problems?"

"Nah. A train was waiting. I got off a stop early and walked, too. Nobody saw."

Vetch seemed pleased. "Hah. I knew she wouldn't leave her place. Didn't even try."

"You were right about her waldo sneaking out the back. I spotted it coming back in, just like you said. I slapped the magnet on it and slipped the bag right over it and that was all there was to it. Pretty good work, huh, Mr. Vetch?"

"Yeah."

"You think she knows we did it?"

"I'll make sure she does. Teach her to rip me, the cunt. Now, beat it, Matthew. I have things to do. I'll call you when another job comes up."

"Where do you want me to put this?" He gestured at Rachne in the bag.

"Just leave it there. I'll take care of it."

"Yes, sir, Mr. Vetch."

Vetch turned away but the kid still stood there.

"What now?" Vetch asked.

"Could I have the bag back? It's the only one I got."

"Beat it!"

The kid looked scared and sidled to the ground-floor exit. Half again the size of Vetch and scared shitless of him. Vetch's main marketable skill was how to make people feel small and stupid.

Vetch left Rachne in the middle of the floor amid the shelves of parts and came up some stairs to the offices on the second-floor mezzanine. He slammed the door. From my angle I couldn't see him through the office window that looked out on the floor, but I could see his shadow on the mezzanine grating. He was using the phone.

It didn't compute. No one would be that nonchalant about who knew how many hundreds of thousands of dollars' worth of diamonds, to leave them lying on the floor like that.

Which meant he didn't know. He hadn't stolen her for the diamonds; it was pure malice that drove him. The threats, the phone calls, the attempt at extortion. All because he liked to make people feel

weak and small and stupid. He'd figured out how to
make a living from being a butthead.

I looked down. My fists were clenching and un-
clenching. It was just as well that I hadn't been able
to come in Golem, and that Vetch was beyond my
grasp for that instant. Because if I'd had the means
I believe I might have killed him.

The inner landing, which led to the mezzanine,
was within reach inside the window but if I used it
all Vetch would have to do was to turn his head and
he'd see me. I slid back out the window, slipped
quietly down the stairs, took a couple of tools out
of my kit, and picked the locks on the door the kid
had used. The door swung open.

When I went inside the mezzanine grating was
directly overhead with the office light and Vetch's
shadow on it. His voice floated out, faintly and with
weird echoes. He was bawling someone out for not
showing up to work last night. The bag was out in
the middle of the floor, possibly within his view,
but in shadow. I took a big breath. Now or never.

I pulled the beanie off my shoulder, fit it onto my
beanlink. White noise filled my head. I pressed the
velcro straps together, hooks to fuzz. My heart
thundered. I crept out and grabbed hold of the bag.
Vetch was no longer at the window—his footsteps
sounded on the floor of the office. He was pacing. I
tugged at the knotted drawstring, cursing under my
breath. Calm, Ruby, calm. Go easy.

The knot came free and I pulled Rachne free of
the bag. A quick glance inside her compartment—
the packet was still there. I'd been half afraid the
kid might have found it. An electromagnet was
stuck to her casing. I grabbed a screwdriver and pried
the magnet loose, pulled out its batteries to deactivate the signal disruptor. The white noise blurred

into image and I was looking at myself looking at myself holding me being held.

With a shudder, I-Rachne looked away from Ruby-my eyes. Ruby-I backed away as I-Rachne struggled up onto my-her ten legs. The office door flew open, and both of me looked up at Vetch, who charged out onto the mezzanine and grabbed the railing.

"Who's out there—?" Then his eyes focused. "You."

"Yeah. Me."

It came out in stereo. When we-I started to move, Vetch ran down the stairs to block our-my path. I-Rachne and Ruby-I spread out, moved toward him on either side.

"Step out of the way," Ruby-I said. He jerked his head toward her-me.

"You seem a little jumpy," I-Rachne said and he looked back at me-her. "Having trouble concentrating?"

"The waldo's mine." He looked back at Ruby-me. "You owe me."

"Somebody should have taught you to read a contract," I-Rachne said.

His eyes slitted. "Yeah? And somebody should have taught you not to fuck with me."

Even junked on adrenaline, my reflexes were sluggish from piloting two bodies at once, and the two sets of visual input made me feel cross-eyed and confused. So I didn't see it coming when, looking Ruby-me right in the eye, he dropped and kicked out sideways, knocking Rachne's legs out from under me-her.

Unbraced and unprepared, I-Rachne collapsed sideways. Ruby-I shoved Vetch from behind to distract him. He stumbled and then turned. Raw hatred in his face, he launched himself at Ruby-me and We-I saw him coming-going but Ruby-I couldn't get out of the way in time. He struck her-me in the chest with his forearms like an offensive football tackle. She-I went to the floor.

He landed with all his weight on my midsection, knocking the wind out of Ruby-me. Then he yanked at the beanie strap, ripping the velcro loose and half choking her-me into the bargain. A few yards away, I-Rachne flailed and kicked, trying to get her legs back under me-her.

Ruby-I grabbed his wrists. A jerk of my head partly dislodged the beanie and I lost contact with Rachne as I-she had almost made it to her feet—regained her as she fell over, rigid. I began to flash in and out of Rachne, flailing and locking, legs scrabbling against the concrete, and caught strobe glimpses of Ruby-me slowly losing the battle to keep Vetch's hands away from the beanie.

With a desperate twist and lurch, Ruby-I got my teeth on his fingers and bit down hard. He cried out—half snarl, half scream. I tasted iron and salt and spat a bloody wad into his face. His pupils contracted even further. I knew he was going to kill me.

"Cunt!"

With one hand he pinned my wrists above my head; the other fist came at my face. She-I dodged but couldn't move far. The blow struck—vision greyed and knuckles tore skin from my cheek. She-I bucked, trying to throw him over my head, and he had to use both hands to keep from going over. But though he's not a big man, he's bigger than me, and no weakling. With one hand he got hold of the beanie's edge.

But I-Rachne had finally gotten her feet back under me-her. I-she charged and grabbed him from behind with a three-fingered Salisbury hand on the back of his neck and the crab claw through his belt. With eight of her metal legs braced on either side of my two flesh ones, I-she hoisted him off Ruby-me like a seventy-kilo sack of junk—just as he dislodged the beanie.

Rachne was well braced when I lost contact. She froze with him suspended in front of her, directly over me, his toes barely brushing my kneecaps. I rolled over out of the way, got onto a knee, picked the beanie up, and shoved it back on before he could swing his weight hard enough to tip her over.

Then I-Rachne dragged him back—legs and arms cartwheeling, cursing a blue streak—against a stanchion, and pinned him there by wrapping several legs around him and several more around the stanchion. After a few seconds he seemed to realize Rachne's compressive and tensile strength significantly outperformed his. He gave up the struggle, heaving great breaths and rolling his eyes.

Ruby-I limped up to him. Vetch was so red in the face and sternum he was almost purple. Ruby-I returned his stare. She-I touched fingers to my cheek. My fingers came away with blood. She-I wiped them across his belly.

"I'm sick of your bullshit, Vetch. I'm tired of your pettiness and your intimidation games. Read the contract. I owe you *nothing*. You're a crook and a nuisance, and I'm done playing nice with you. If you ever try something like this again I swear I'll bam the shit out of you."

He looked down at the bloody fingerprints on his abdomen and when he looked up at my face again, fear glinted in his eyes.

"All right," he said. "All right."

I-Rachne held him till Ruby-I had reached the exit, then dropped him and walked over to join Ruby-me

at the door. He grabbed the stanchion for support.
When we-I looked back, he gave Ruby-me a concil-
iatory grin.

"No hard feelings," he said. "Really."

That just made me want to choke him some more.
"Don't count on it."

Rich, Rich,
Filthy Rich

RACHNE and I caught the next monorail train back
and got home shortly after sunrise. Melissa hadn't
come back yet.

After pressing a seal patch to my cheekbone to
sterilize the cut and hide the spreading, yellow-green
bruise, I reactivated Rachne and we-I went over to
the squish-couch. I pulled the beanie off, looked at
my little spider waldo with her camera platform,
the two spheroid sections of her chassis, her spindly
legs. I gave her an affectionate smile.

"Old woman, you may need an overhaul but you
were really something today."

Then I removed the envelope and taped bundle
from her compartment and sank into my squish-
couch. The envelope I dropped across my knees. I
picked the diamonds out of the Teflon tape one at
a time, to roll them between my fingers and hold
them up to the incandescent light of the amp-lamp
clamped onto the control panel above my head.

There were eight, the smallest pair at least a carat
in size and the largest closer to four, if I was to
hazard a guess. All faceted, rainbow fire-trapping

prisms set in red gold; I didn't have a clue what they were worth but it must have been a lot.

Staring at them, it finally began to register on me: I'm rich now. Rich enough to buy an interface upgrade, rich enough to buy a new waldo—or perhaps to retrofit faithful Golem, loyal Rachne. Rich enough not to have to starve and beg between jobs, to afford a real air conditioner, even an envie cool suit, and be free to leave my house by day and not be cooked to death. Rich enough to buy sanity and safety. Eight white stones.

And there was the envelope. I flashed on a memory of the old man's hands clutching it to his chest. It was something more precious to him even than diamonds.

Curiosity got the better of me. I rolled the diamonds carefully in a hanky, set them aside, and then picked up the envelope. The big red letters stamped across the front said "PERSONAL AND CONFIDENTIAL—Sidra Nasser." I ripped open the envelope with a screwdriver, which violated the opening instructions printed in reflective letters across the back seam. Beads of gelpaper insulation spilled from the envelope's torn lips and, as they touched air turned to oily liquid and trickled over my thighs.

I reached into the envelope and touched a piece of paper, something angular on a chain, and a second, smaller envelope. I pulled them out.

The paper was a note and the angular thing on a chain, a bronze cross. The smaller envelope had some Arabic writing on it, along with an official-looking seal, and it was bound with a ribbon. The note was in English. It read:

    Dear Sidra,
      I have attempted to visit you two times

now, but the sentinels of your circle of worship have refused me entrance to speak with you. They say you don't want to see me. I suppose I can understand.

One cannot take back words once they have been spoken. I wish to God I could. After my heart troubles last fall I realize how fleeting life is and how important you are to me.

My will includes you once more. I've enclosed an official, signed copy of the will, witnessed by Rachel's cousin Jehenna and also Ibrahim Hanna, whom you may remember from our summer vacations in Aswan. Rachel has the other copy and will file it with our legal counsel. The cross is yours, too, as I promised when you were a boy.

You're now my executor. If it is still your wish to turn your share of the inheritance over to the leaders of your pagan faith, I hope you will reconsider. But let me not resurrect that specter now. Whatever you decide I will accept.

I want to see you again. Fifteen years is long enough; it is too long. The man who delivers this to you has been told to escort you, should you wish to accompany him now, or to provide you with information on how to reach me, should you need time to think.

I was a stubborn old fool. Forgive me.

The signature was an illegible scrawl.

The other envelope must have held the will. I didn't particularly care what he'd willed and to who; it for sure wasn't me, and by now I was feeling funny enough about opening the big envelope. So I shoved the small envelope back into the bigger one, along with the cross and the note. Then I put Rachne away in the basement, and came back and looked out the window for a while.

Haze, smoke, and heat waves blurred the air. The crowds had abandoned the streets in the past half hour; not even the neighborhood dogs were out. I tapped fingers on the windowpane and found the glass hot to the touch. It had to be 125 degrees out there, and summer was weeks away.

I unfolded the hanky and looked at the diamonds again, then tucked them in the hip pocket of my cutoffs. My dad, I'd hated him. When I was sixteen I'd vowed never to be a crook like him. Like Vetch.

But it wasn't as if there was only one copy of the will. And they were so wealthy they weren't going to miss those diamonds—their fortune gained and lost more than the worth of those diamonds every weekday in the stock market.

Those diamonds weren't stolen; they were salvage. A reward for recovering the old man's body, which would never have been found in the wreckage if not for me. In fact, he probably would have given me the diamonds, if he'd lived. I pictured him drawing his last breaths in my-Golem's arms, and pressing the diamonds into Golem's telescoper claw. "Take them, Ruby. You deserve them. Don't feel bad for me. You did your best."

It was a good scene, so vivid and realistic that I found myself getting all choked up and grateful. I wiped at my eyes.

My glance fell on the envelope. That was the nuisance factor. If I'd just left that in his cool suit everything would have been fine. But he'd clutched it like it was so valuable.

I thought about old Dr. Nasser's wife—Rachel, was it? Rachel Karam. Thought about that look in her eyes when she'd asked what they had recovered from the yacht, the flickering glance she'd given me. She knew I'd taken the diamonds.

Then it hit me. In the letter the old man had said she had the only other copy of the will. So maybe it wasn't the *diamonds* she'd wanted to stay lost. Maybe she figured losing the diamonds was a small price to pay for the loss of an inconvenient will.

But what about the two who had witnessed the letter, the Jehenna and Ibrahim he'd mentioned? Surely they wouldn't ignore Nasser's wish to reinherit his own son. Maybe they didn't know the terms of the will. People didn't always know these things. Or had she paid them off, too?

Guesses, all guesses. But I had this feeling in my gut. She'd known what she was doing, what she was offering me. . . .

With a sigh, I scratched at my hair, rubbed my gritty eyes. I hadn't gotten half the sleep I needed over the last three days and I felt like every minute of it. I ached all over from my fight with Vetch. My week's nonpotable quota was mostly blown, too, so I couldn't wash off all the street grunge. Even this filthy I could sleep, though—could I ever.

But first a couple of jellophone calls, to find a merchant who wouldn't cheat me on my diamonds. And, out of curiosity, a quick login to the civic bulletin board, for a glance at the obits to see when and where the burial was. Just out of curiosity. Poor old guy.

THE SCREAMER, AGAIN

AFTER a meager splash bath with a washrag and a few inches of tepid water in the sink, I went to bed early, before noon. That time when I heard the screaming again I knew it couldn't be real. It *still* kept me awake.

SHE LOVES ME

A weight settled on my bed. I woke with a start and struggled the sheet down, sheathed in sweat.

"Who is it?"

A dark silhouette blocked the strobing lights that shone through the curtains. The air was hot, close and still; the air conditioner had stopped working again. The silhouette bent down and buried its head in my lap, and I knew from the spice scent of her perfume who it was.

"I'm sorry, Rube."

I released my breath and took another. Then I reached out and touched the head in my lap.

"Me, too," I said.

THE LIGHT
SLOWLY DAWNS

So what the hell; nothing good was on the JV, using the blink-beanie made me feel guilty, and I couldn't do much else on a Sunday morning. So I geared Tiger up—Rachne being too conspicuous—and went to a funeral.

The ceremony started at five-thirty, shortly before sunrise, at the American Reformed Coptic Church in Brooklyn, a venerable structure that used to be Episcopalian and holds easily a few thousand people. And it was a good thing, too, because the turnout was standing room only. When I-Tiger rolled up to the steps of the church at 5:06, the two ushers at the doors—who bulged out of their cool suits like Egyptian linebackers and from my-Tiger's perspective towered several stories into the sky—were checking people's invites. A whole crowd of people milled around in the street and on the sidewalk, waiting to get in.

A lot of them got turned away at the door, mostly the press. I spotted the mayor and several celebs. The ushers let them through, naturally. I wondered what they'd do to a toy tank. Probably step on me. But hell if I wasn't going to try.

I-Tiger dodged heels, sandals, sneakers, and boots the size of meat lockers to the steps. Then I-he slid his taloned arms from their sheaths and planted them on the ground, turned on the spring motor, and started to rise, teetering on the arm stilts. The edge of the first step appeared at the top edge of my vision and gradually lowered till it was beneath my line of sight.

I put Tiger's purple plastic tractor treads in gear and then started to rock by contracting and relaxing his talons. I-he fell forward and retracted the arms, landed with a jarring bump, and teetered on the edge of the step before the treads grabbed hold of the concrete and carried me-him forward to safety at the base of the second step.

My gain was short-lived; the toe of a descending boot caught and lifted me-Tiger into the air. The world fell away, tumbling, and returned. With a crunch, I-he landed on his back on the asphalt and rocked to and fro like an upended turtle.

Annoying, but not a disaster. A systems check showed no damage; Tiger was built as a trainer waldo and was hardy as all get-out. With his arms and treads it was only seconds before I-he had righted myself-him. This time I scouted out an area less crowded. I-Tiger splashed through the gutter, climbed the curb, dodged feet, and struggled back up the five steps.

As I-Tiger neared the wooden doors the Egyptian usher-guards loomed overhead like monster statues. I downshifted to Tiger's lowest gear ratio and accelerated, thinking, don't look down, guys.

They didn't have to. The instant I-Tiger crossed the threshold, a bell started chiming somewhere. Antiwaldo security systems. I flooded Tiger's systems with power and I-he veered away from the feet in the way, making for the chapel door.

The chase was short. A massive hand closed around me, and I barely had time to register the dark-and-orange of sunlight through flesh before the world appeared, tumbling again, and a baritone voice said, "No press allowed!"

Humiliating. As before, though, I-Tiger landed unhurt. I-he scrabbled back upright and made my-his slow and painful way back through the gutter, up onto the curb and up the steps. By this time the crowds had thinned out and they were closing the big double doors. The two usher-guards stood in front of it with their arms folded.

A glance around told me that I-Tiger wasn't the only waldo, nor the only one refused entrance; an assortment of different-sized boxes, gadgets, and bugsy-things hummed and buzzed and hovered around the doors amid the human reporters, television crews, vans, cameras, distance microphones, and the like. So I hung around outside with the press.

I could have looked for a side entrance, but breaking and entering wasn't too schick at a man's funeral. So I gave up the effort and positioned myself-Tiger near a window. I tinkered with Tiger's hearing focus and direction until I could make out someone's voice—the minister's, droning on about old Nasser's accomplishments.

There were lots of boo-hoos and noise like that. They did the same thing at my dad's funeral, brought in a mystic old fart who knew nothing about Dad to fling holy water and make up a bunch of lies about what a family man he was, and to assure us all that he was up there smiling down on us so we shouldn't feel bad that he'd junked himself out on rage one too many times and had a brain hemorrhage in the middle of one of his dish-breaking rampages.

Maybe all that stuff about Nasser was true. If it was, he deserved sainthood or something. They left out the part about how he'd tossed his son out and Christ knows what else he did. Funerals piss me off.

But I didn't have the heart to stay mad at the old man. He hadn't asked to be crushed in a bombed-out building. So I-Tiger bumped around on the sidewalk outside the stained glass and hewn blocks with the rest of the rejects and bided my time.

Eventually the usher-guards received some signal and opened the doors of the church. The press—and I-Tiger—crowded around.

The minister came out first, an oldish jowly man with yellowed skin, a large nose, and dark, deep-set eyes, in a black robe with a hooded cowl. The IR plume that billowed out behind him must have been from a hidden cool vest. He had white linens draped over his arms and around his neck, and he swung a brass thurifer on a chain in a slow and steady rhythm. At the peak of each swing a puff of smoke appeared. A couple of light-skinned guys in tasteful pin-striped cool suits followed him, mortuary types, each with his hands clasped in front of him, each wearing a patronizing smirk that was probably supposed to be serene.

Next the pallbearers came carrying a coffin of mahogany and silver covered with wreaths of flowers that were only just starting to wilt. I stared. *Man* was this guy loaded.

Then came the old man's wife, Rachel, with a younger female companion at her arm who looked a bit like her only less made-over. Rachel wore not a cool suit but a plain black dress in the *natureil* fashion, made of gauze layers with loose sleeves and a filmy black shawl over her head. She had no cool-vest plume, either. My respect for her went up. It was 114 degrees Fahrenheit and 82 percent humidity this morning.

A lot of the people who filed out were crying. I spotted Captain Nanopoulos, looking self-possessed, if a little preoccupied. Her sandaled foot went down next to me-Tiger and I had to resist the urge to make a crack or call out a greeting.

The minister and the pallbearers-with-coffin entered the cemetery through its wrought-iron gate, followed by old Nasser's wife Rachel, her companions, and a tall, athletic-looking man maybe a few years older than me, about thirty or so, in the burlap robes of a Forest Veils monastic novitiate. His eyes looked raw with shock and his head was shaved. That had to be Sidra—he was the only young black male who was granted entry to the burial. I wondered whether he had refused the role of pallbearer or whether Rachel had simply not asked him. Wondered whether he cared.

The burial was family and close friends only; the obit had said so. Still, it was a shock to see the guards at the gate turn away the mayor and the film and stage stars. They did let Nanopoulos in, which pissed me off again. I'd busted my ass and ruined my Golem trying to rescue him, and it was some cop who got to go to his funeral.

Others I didn't recognize also entered, including a dozen or so women with veiled faces dressed in black gowns who entered the cemetery in pairs, fingers over their mouths under the veils. They swayed as they walked and wailed almost like the cries of sea birds—a sorrowful, minor-key song. Their cries gave me chills; it was too much like how the screamer sounded.

Most of the rest who entered wore their wealth like advert strips: cool suits, polymer-treated hair, face paint and hair glows and sparkles. Maybe they'd dressed down from their usual for the funeral, but it sure didn't show to my eyes. Then the guards closed the gates and fended off the people and waldos who crowded up to the wall of rock and iron.

Just down from the cemetery was an abandoned tennis court; I'd seen it on my way over. I-Tiger broke away from the crowd, entered the court, and bumped across the cracked concrete to the backstop, a thirty-foot fence of chain link. None of the press had followed me. I-Tiger extended his arms, grabbed hold, and began to climb.

Tiger's talons weren't designed for climbing fences and the angle was bad, but I put my years of experience with Golem to good use. I-Tiger scrambled, clunked, and ratcheted up the chain link at an agonizing crawl: a crippled, bowlegged mechanical rodent.

From about twenty-two feet up the burial was visible. I-Tiger zoomed in.

A concrete structure—a tomb, I guess you'd call it—was built into the ground on a small rise, obscured from the road by a stand of palm trees. The pallbearers were lowering the coffin onto a chrome-plated, robotic gurney before the tomb. The gurney was mounted on some violently green astro-turf put there to hide the piles of fresh dirt. The mourners were seating themselves with their backs to me on antique walnut chairs with black velvet-cushioned seats, on a carpet of plush crimson that had been spread before the coffin.

The minister stood between the coffin and the tomb with his head bowed and a Bible in his hands, and the two men in pin-striped cool suits, attempting to be discreet, moved over to flank him. The women in black stood to the side, still trilling, wailing and moaning.

The minister looked up at the people then, with a look of faint surprise like he'd thought he was

alone. Then he lifted a hand and the women in black
fell silent. He lifted one of the linens draped over
his sleeves, kissed it, and then laid it on the coffin.
Then he opened his Bible, licked a finger, and flipped
a page or two. He read, glancing up occasionally and
holding his place with the finger. I tuned and focused
Tiger's hearing.

He read the "Yea, though I walk through the val-
ley of the shadow" scripture—always a popular fa-
vorite at funerals. Then he flipped pages again.

"Let us pray," he said. Heads bowed. "Seven arch-
angels stand glorifying the Almighty and serving the
hidden Mystery. . . ."

I scanned the mourners while he went on. Nanopoulos acted like she was really paying attention
to the minister, but Rachel kept glancing back at
Sidra, like she couldn't resist. I thought it was pretty
rude, she being the deceased's wife and all.

". . . the four living creatures bearing the chariot
of God," he said, ". . . Heaven and Earth . . . praise
him without ceasing . . . Holy is the Almighty; give
rest to the departed. Holy is the Immortal; bless
thine inheritance. . . . Holy, holy, holy . . . Heaven
and earth are full of thy glory. Intercede for us O
angels our guardians, and all heavenly hosts, that
our sins may be forgiven."

Sidra sat in a chair near the back. At the words
"that our sins may be forgiven," he shot the minister a single, dreadful look. He'd chosen a seat far
from Rachel and didn't look at her; I couldn't figure
out whether her glances were aggressive or whether
she was trying to catch his attention.

I-Tiger zoomed on Sidra. His black skin was grey
with pallor, and he swallowed hard a couple of
times. His fists clenched and unclenched in his robe.

After the minister finished reading, one of the

men in the pin-striped cool suits came up and touched a button on the chrome gurney. Steel talons gripped the coffin, and the gurney rolled into the darkness of the tomb. With Tiger's IR I-he watched the gurney slide the coffin onto a concrete slab at the tomb's side. The minister was talking again.

". . . it is written, the Lord is my light and my salvation. Yes, Lord, draw me to thyself. Thou art a faithful God, a merciful Father, the giver of all that is good, and the instructor of the heart."

The gurney rolled back out and hunkered down in its original place. The minister closed his book with rather too loud a noise, and said, "May the soul of Youhanna Nasser rest in peace in the kingdom of our merciful Father in heaven, now and forever more. Go in peace and remember him. Amen."

"Amen," everybody else muttered.

As if on cue, the women in black started wailing again. The rest of the mourners stood. Rachel walked up to the tomb, looked inside it for a second, and then said something in Arabic, I guess it was. Then she turned to bury her face against the shoulder of her companion. Except for the women in black, who remained at the tomb, wailing enthusiastically, the other mourners wandered away, talking quietly or silent.

A short distance away Rachel and her companion turned to watch Sidra. He had stayed seated, looking at the unfinished tomb. Then he stood up and strode in my general direction, looking, if anything, angry.

I-Tiger picked up a faint, "Go after him, Jehenna"; Rachel gave her companion a nudge and the younger woman ran after Sidra. Then Rachel dried her eyes, turning to the group that had gathered to speak to her.

It took me a while to locate Sidra and the woman, Jehenna, among the trees and tombs. They were moving more toward the back of the cemetery now, side by side, disappearing and reappearing among the palm fronds and stone tombs and statues of angels.

"She means it," Jehenna said.

He held up a hand like a traffic cop, with a sharp shake of his head.

"Don't," he said, and Jehenna closed her mouth on what she'd been about to say. "Don't lie to me. I don't know what you two are trying to prove but I know quite well how much Rachel hates me."

"You're wrong, Sid."

He gave her a raised eyebrow. "Oh, am I?"

"Yes. She resented you once. But it's ancient history now. Everyone's forgiven and forgotten those days but you. Why can't you believe that?"

He gave her a skeptical look.

"Listen to me." She touched his arm. "She sent me to you. She wants you there to help mourn Youhanna, and so do I."

"I can mourn as easily with the people of my faith."

"They never knew him."

"No, but they know me."

"They're not family!"

"They are *my* family."

Jehenna templed her hands and pressed them against her lips, studying his face. "All right, then, come for another reason. She's going to sell Aïn el Baraka. Come help us put the house in order."

He looked shocked. Then he shook his head. "Why are you going to all this trouble? Why don't you leave me alone?"

"I told you. We want to make peace."

"Why should I help you sort through *his* things? Hire help, if you need it."

Silence followed. I couldn't tell what it meant because they had moved behind a blur of green palms and bleached-white tombs. When they didn't appear where their trajectory should have led them I knew I'd lost them.

Shit. I cranked Tiger's volume up and scanned . . . nothing but the chirps and rustlings of graveyard birds and rodents. They must have stopped moving or gone off in another direction.

A flicker of movement caught my eye amid the palm leaves near where they'd first disappeared. I honed in—and got Jehenna's voice like ice picks, stabbing right into the ears. I nearly levitated—I yanked the lead out and was home again, thrashing, my own yell still echoing in my ears. Melissa came out of the kitchen holding a soapy plate in dripping hands, a questioning look on her face.

I gave her a rather sickly smile. "Volume too high."

She shook her head at me, looking mildly disgusted, and went back into the kitchen. Trembling, I lowered the volume manually with a flick of the control switches, and then plugged back in.

". . . see that you receive something," Jehenna was saying. "She tried to get Youhanna to change his will to include you, you know, near the end."

It took a second for me to understand her remark. Then I got mad. You liar, I thought. He did change his will. He changed it.

By this time they had reappeared. Sidra gave her a hooded look. "I don't need his money. I have my faith to sustain me."

"You deserve to receive something to remember your father by."

He said nothing but his lips were trembling.

"You owe it to him," she said. "Come and spend some time with the family, mourning him properly."

"He kicked me out!"

"Yes, and when he tried to reconcile with you, *you* shut *him* out. Whose fault is that?"

God damn you, I thought. He is in his father's will and you know it.

Sidra, of course, couldn't hear me. He gave Jehenna the same ghastly look he'd given the priest earlier. Then he seemed to deflate. He covered his face.

"Not in his will?" Sidra said. His voice wavered.

"Not in his heart." He wiped at his eyes and drew a breath. While his head was lowered she watched him like a cat waiting for the bug to move. Then he lifted his head and met her eyes.

"All right, then. Tell Rachel I'll come tonight. I need a few hours to go back to the monastery to inform them, and pack some things—"

"No." At his look, she softened the word. "No need. We have everything you need at Aïn el Baraka. Call your people from the house. Take the limo with us. Everything's arranged."

They headed back toward the front of the cemetery. Meanwhile, I-Tiger clung to the wire like a cat stuck up a pole while I tired to figure out how to get down. I-Tiger tried a couple of angles and holds, but it plain wasn't going to work.

What the hell, I thought. I-Tiger retracted his arms. The world fell up and I-he hit the concrete hard enough to bounce twice.

The sun, engorged on smog and ozone-laden haze,

had slipped above the tiled roof of the church by the time I-Tiger had struggled onto his treads and rolled back out to the street. The crowds outside the cemetery were thinning; collocars choked the road and a shouting chorus of car horns had begun. A dust devil spun down the street and I couldn't tell if those screams I heard were the cries of the women in black or if I was imagining things again.

Well, it wasn't my problem. But her lies really burned me. *Everything's arranged.* I'll just bet it is, I thought. I'll bet you've taken care of every little thing.

MELISSA RECEIVES
A VISITOR

THE intercom buzzed. That was a shock. It was ten A.M., late for fringe folk to be out, and neither of us had visitors very often in any event.

"You expecting someone?" I asked Melissa. She'd gone back to bed after finishing the dishes. Now she muttered something that sounded like, "marrr mifff awone," and heaved herself over like she was having a petit mal seizure.

The bell went off again.

"Melissa?"

She stuffed the edges of her pillow around her face. It had to be for her, but I tossed my book aside anyhow, struggled out of the squish-couch, and pressed the button on the intercom by the door.

Darian Vetch's face appeared in the little b/w TV screen, looking smug. I barely stifled a snarl.

"What do you want?"

"I'm here to see Melissa."

"The hell you are."

He grinned. "She's expecting me. Ask her."

I looked back at her on her bed, then at Vetch again. I smiled back, but my guts were churning. He had to be joking. He had better be.

"Sorry. She's gone out with some other jerk. You've been stood up."

"Ruby, what are you doing? Of course I'm here." Melissa shoved me out of the way, rubbing her eyes, baring her tits to Vetch. I wanted to scream.

"I'm here, Dare, come on up."

She pressed the outer-door latch-release button next to the viewer screen. Then she pulled a mini-length, emerald-green kimono with a gold and crimson dragon on the back from her bed knob and put it on. Tying the sash, she stumbled into the kitchen and dug around in the refrigerator for a raw egg to put in her orange juice.

"Aw, shit," she said, eyeing the clock while she blended the Orange Julius. "I forgot about him."

I leaned on the doorjamb. She poured her snack from the blender into a glass and looked out the window past the ivy plant above the sink as she drank it. In the sunlight she looked tousled, graceful, sleepy, and magnificent. I felt as if she'd just shoved a foot-long dagger of glass deep into my diaphragm.

She wiped her OJ mustache off and smiled at me.

"I forgot to tell you, honey, I have a date. I'll probably be gone through the evening. 'kay?"

I shook my head, found my voice. "He's no good, Liss. I know him."

The doorbell rang. She gave me a puzzled look and started past. I grabbed her arm.

"I mean it. Cancel your date."

She jerked her arm loose. "Fuck off. I'm sick of your jealous fits."

"It's not jealousy." I ran past her and blocked the front door before she could open it. The bell rang again. "I've known him for over a year. He has the morals of a reptile. He's been trying to steal from me."

She stood there and looked at me till my insides started to quiver. The bell was ringing continuously now, jarringly. "You're not my mother and you have no right to interfere with my life. Get out of the way."

I drew a breath. "All right, then, go out with him. But no way in hell he's coming into my apartment."

The look in her eyes of anger and betrayal twisted the dagger she'd buried in my chest. The look said, *my* apartment? It had been hers alone for years, before she took me in and saved me from the streets, when T-M had given me the boot.

"Get out of the way," she said again.

I couldn't face that look down. So I got out of the way. Enough for her to pull the door open and let Vetch inside.

He kissed Melissa, hard, open-mouthed, with a hand like a vise on the back of her neck, and I couldn't help but watch. I felt like I'd put down roots, there behind the door. Melissa giggled and poked him in the stomach.

"Wow. You sure know how to say hello. I have to change—have a seat." Melissa gestured at her lounge lizard and started to dig through her half of the closet, next to the bathroom.

Vetch sauntered inside, grinning over his shoulder at me, and wandered around the apt giving everything a long look. He saw Rachne over by my bed; her compartment door was still open. He noticed that and gave me a look of sudden comprehension.

That was good for a spike of nervousness. But even if he had just guessed lucky, that Rachne had had some salvage when he'd grabbed her, he'd never guess what it had been. I gave him a shrug.

Melissa drew some clothing out of the closet, blew Vetch a kiss, and then disappeared into the bathroom. As soon as the door closed I crossed over to him and said, softly so Melissa wouldn't overhear, "You'll leave her alone if you know what's good for you."

Vetch spread his hands. "Like I said, no hard feelings. I'm just looking for some good times, that's all. I didn't even know you two were roomies when Mel and I met yesterday."

Like hell. But I couldn't prove anything. So I just stood there, arms folded, and glowered at him until Melissa came back out in her tank top, wearing glow paints, gauze harem pants shot through with metal threads, her hair piled up. She grabbed a wrap and pulled him out the door, laughing. I shut the door on them as his arm went around her waist and he nuzzled her neck.

I sank back into my squish-couch and cried for a while. Then I put Rachne away downstairs, did the dishes, and then watched soaps on the jello-tube and drank the last of the beer.

INTERLUDE

THE screamer's wail that night seemed more like a grieving friend than an accuser. I lay, hand pillowing my head, and listened, watching the reflections of the changing fluorescents outside, and thinking of Melissa and Vetch together.

Around midnight when she came in I pretended to be asleep. A half hour later when I got up to go out she pretended to be asleep.

The outer door caused me barely a moment's hesitation. I guess you'd call it progress.

SERIOUS SHIT

THE electronic lock buzzed and I pushed the door inward. The air inside Hammond & Hammond, Jewelers, Ltd., stirred, noticeably less hot and oppressive than the night air outside, bitter, smelling of solvents and must.

The room's only light spilled from glass cases that encircled the walls. A white man with splotches on his forehead pushed the sleeves of his baggy linen shirt above his elbows and flipped up the lenses of his jeweler's specs to look at me. He sat behind one of the glass cases, wearing a bow tie of grey paisley silk and a pin-striped cool vest. His gaunt, beak-nosed face was lit up from below, which made him look kind of jade, satanic even, and it was all I could do to stay rooted.

"Yes?" he said after a pause. "What can I do for you?"

Hammond & Hammond were reputable diamond merchants, small volume, and most importantly, Bostonian. I'd decided no way I was going to try to sell the diamonds to a New York merchant. Never mind what cheats New York merchants can be; I didn't want anyone in town connecting me with the diamonds.

I was probably overdoing it with the caution. After the talk between Jehenna and Sidra I knew without a doubt that Rachel Karam had meant the diamonds to be a payoff and that she hadn't reported them missing. But I wasn't about to rely on her continued goodwill.

A bullet train, round-trip, New York to Boston, took fifty-four minutes each way and cost $264. That left $17.42 in my account, which would buy me a dry scone and lemon in my iced tea. And if Calen didn't have the rent today he'd have Melissa's and my ass. This deal had better go down or I was in serious shit.

I came up and leaned on the counter. The jeweler frowned at me, eyebrows bristling. The way he perched on his stool he reminded me of a carrion bird, hunched over his elbows on a wooden worktable whose surface was worn and gouged, scattered with bits of wax and slivers of gold. The table had a miniature vise mounted on it, which held a clear, dark green, faceted jewel in a gold setting. A cabinet with many tiny drawers of transparent plastic sat at the back. An abstract shape in red wax, a blue plastic squeeze bottle, and several interesting-looking tools lay on the table.

"Hi." My voice quavered. Damn it. "I need some assistance."

"Please don't lean on the counter," he said, still frowning, and pointed to a sign with small, neat letters by my elbow: DO NOT LEAN ON THE COUNTER.

"Oops." I removed my elbows from the counter with an apologetic grimace and unfolded the handkerchief to reveal the smallest pair of diamonds. I'd hidden the rest in a drain beneath my tool cabinet, and had added the cross and the will for good measure. That screamer was making me jumpy as hell. Or maybe it was my guilty conscience. I was getting downright paranoid.

"I need to know what these are worth."

The jeweler's frown disappeared. He flipped his magnifier specs down, turning his eyes to enormous, blue ceramic marbles, and with his pincers gripped and lifted one of the diamonds. When he swung his light over it, the reflections in the stone burned my eyes like pinpoint lasers. Rainbow-tinged flecks of light dotted his face. He didn't look nearly so intimidating and vulturelike without the frown. He took a reading from the LCD on his pincer handle, then set the first one down.

"One-point-one-two carats," he said, and picked up the second one. "And one-point-one-one. Now I should like a moment to verify that they are natural stones and to examine their clarity, color, and brilliance."

I caught my breath while his balding head bent over them. Noises ensued: mmms and ahs and oh?s. His knobbly hands had stains on them. He laid each diamond in a box, sealed it, and took readings from the LCD displays on the outside.

"The carbon twelve-thirteen-fourteen ratios indicate that these are natural stones," he said. "Outstanding quality, too. Outstanding." Then his hand flipped up the magnifying lenses again, and he gave me a speckled blue, inquisitive look.

I adjusted the hood of my drape—I'd pinned it with at least ten fasteners to keep it from slipping off and exposing my beanjack, but couldn't help being paranoid about it anyway—and said, "They're an heirloom."

I managed to say this without stammering, mostly because I'd practiced on the bullet train down. Even in my one nice outfit, my tangerine drape with the garnet brooch and my hair polymer-waxed in short ringlets and some of Melissa's paints tastefully applied to face and neck (which not coincidentally hid the cut and ever darkening bruise on my cheek), I felt cheap and unconvincing. But I figured an ounce of moxie can overpower a ton of common sense. Besides, for disguise, the bird-of-paradise swirls of tangerine and emerald sparkling on my forehead, eyelids, cheeks, and chin did even better duty than a cool mask.

"I need to insure them," I added. "I wanted an outside opinion before I went to the insurer."

"Ah, well. Hmmm. Of course." The eyebrows, bushy mustachios over his eyes, went up and down a couple of times while he examined the diamonds through his lenses again. I eyed his displays distractedly and chewed my cuticle. Say, I thought, can I borrow your bathroom? I need to throw up.

"Insure them for at least one hundred eighty thousand apiece," he said finally. "That would be replacement cost. The insurance company's appraiser will give you a more exact figure, but anything less than that and you'd be unable to replace them at retail."

A breath dragged through my teeth. He smiled at my gape-mouthed stare and pursed his fleshy lips.

"They're absolutely flawless, young woman, as clear and brilliant and colorless as you'll find anywhere in a natural stone. Free of impurities or cloudiness of any kind. And the cut is excellent. Top caliber. I haven't seen work this good in a long time. You won't have any trouble insuring them at that price."

"But what if I were to sell them—"

I broke off when he started nodding. "I was coming to that. If you were to sell them you'd get a good deal less than three hundred sixty thousand—unless you were lucky enough to find a private buyer willing to pay retail price for them."

That was a pretty clear way of telling me which of us would be making the profit in a transaction. After a moment I said, "If I wanted to exchange them for one double the size—of the same quality—"

He was shaking his head already, anticipating my question. "You couldn't, not without paying more. The larger they are, the more rare they are, so the price goes up more rapidly than the size.

"A two-carat stone of this quality would be—I'd estimate, oh, close to half a million dollars, retail. Possibly more."

Which meant I owned several million dollars' worth of diamonds. Holy shit—I'd been carrying them in a hanky like they were pebbles.

The band of muscles around my chest tightened till I could barely breathe. I held out the hanky with a trembling hand. He gave me a smile. My heart lurched when he reached under his counter—I half expected a gun—but he brought out a jewel box, a black matte vinyl job with "Hammond & Hammond, Jewelers, Ltd." scrolled on top in gold letters and folds of black velvet on the inside.

He popped the lid and dropped the diamonds onto the velvet. When he pressed the box into my hand his face had a rather wistful look. A good sign. I closed a fist around the box and swallowed.

"Good night, then," he said, flipped his lenses down, and turned back to the green jewel in the vise.

I leaned forward on my toes and cleared my throat. "Would you, perhaps—"

"Yes?"

"I was wondering whether you'd be interested in making an offer."

He raised his formidable eyebrows at me and pushed out his lower lip till it looked like a blister about to pop. "Indeed? Well, Ms.—"

I'd prepared for that one. "Jamison."

"—Ms. Jamison, I'd say yes, we'd be interested in discussing a possible sale. You understand, of course, that we'd be unable to give you anything close to the retail price I quoted . . . otherwise we'd have no real incentive to buy them, because we'd be tying up capital without being able to make a profit on the sale."

"Of course not," I said. I opened my hand again, flipped the box open, and set it down on the counter in front of him. "So what kind of price *would* you offer for diamonds of this high a quality?"

He gave me a wry look, then sucked his lip back in and glanced at the diamonds with a slight frown. He wanted them; I could tell.

"Oh, I don't know," he said, and picked up the diamonds to scrutinize them.

"They go well as a pair," I said, "don't they? I

expect that makes them more valuable than each would be separately."

"Mmmm. Could be." He dropped them back in the box, set it down just beyond my fingertips, and met my gaze. "What would you be wanting for them?"

I chewed my cuticle again. I know how to drive a bargain, but I know junk a lot better than I know diamonds. Besides, I hate bargaining in person. When I deal with salvage clients it's always in waldo—they can't read me that way. If I could have gotten away with it this time I would have, but there was no quicker and better way to be IDed than to teeter in on Rachne's legs. Or worse, to come in my poor Golem. So I was stuck with my own scared and trembling body for one of the most important deals I'd ever be likely to strike.

Moxie. Think moxie.

"Certainly I can understand your wanting to make a profit," I said. "On the other hand, I wouldn't want to dishonor the memory of my great aunt by selling her diamonds at a bargain-basement price. She brought them with her from Europe, you know." I pinched my lip and pretended to mull things over, looking at the diamonds. "You quoted three hundred sixty kay for the two of them. I'll let them go for three hundred kay. You'll make sixty thousand, free and clear."

He seemed alarmed. "No, no. You clearly don't understand the diamond business. That low a profit is not even worth considering. Diamonds in that price range do not turn over quickly. To tie up so much capital for such a marginal profit would be insane—and who knows what the diamond market will do before they sell? No, we couldn't possibly give you more than one hundred thousand for the two of them."

I choked on an outraged noise. "Excuse me—I can't have heard you right. One hundred thousand—that's robbery!" I'd found my barter voice; that last came out without even a twitch of an eyelid. "I couldn't possibly take less than two hundred eighty kay."

He sighed, much put upon. "One fifty."

"Two fifty."

He studied me for a moment, looking thoughtful. "You drive a hard bargain, young woman."

"I owe it to the memory of Aunt Tillie, sir. She'd do back flips in her grave if she thought I'd taken less than half what they're worth."

He sighed again and his glance went to the diamonds. He was trying to be chill, but he wanted them.

"One hundred eighty," he said reluctantly, "and my partner will contract ulcers when I tell him."

I refrained with great effort from chewing my lip. Christ, Ruby, take it! But I had a drop of Scottish blood in my veins.

"I couldn't take a penny less than two hundred kay, sir."

He shook his head, harried and victimized. Then he blew air out with his cheeks puffed up; I'd read him right. "Let's split the difference. One hundred ninety thousand dollars for the two of them. That's the best I can do for you."

I gave the diamonds a wistful good-bye, and pushed the box toward him. "You just bought yourself some diamonds, sir."

A grin spread across his face; he poured the diamonds into his hands and rolled them between his fingers. "Give me your account number and I'll transfer the funds immediately."

"Um, actually," I said, "I'd prefer cash."

Something changed in his face. "We don't deal in cash."

My stomach sank like a lump of lead in water. But I stoked my moxie, put on an innocent expression, and met his eyes.

"I don't want my parents to know I'm selling Aunt Tillie's diamonds," I said. "Don't get me wrong; they're mine to sell. But if my parents knew they'd insist on buying back the diamonds and paying my bills for me and I don't want to owe them—"

But he was shaking his head. He dropped the diamonds back into the box and there was a look of finality on his face.

"I'm sorry, Ms. Jamison, but I'm afraid I can't help you. First you tell me you need a price for insurance purposes, then you offer to sell the diamonds, then you'll only take cash. That sort of thing—well, we bank on our reputation and we can't afford trouble. You'll have to take your business elsewhere."

"What—?"

"Take your business elsewhere." He turned back to his table.

With a curse and a glare that was lost on him, I snatched up the diamonds. I slammed the door open on the way out, hoping it would break.

Heat slapped me in the face and burned like caustic in my sinuses and throat; I dodged cars across the street, matched speed with the sidewalk that headed into the downtown environment canopy, and jumped on, shoving my way in among the jostling crowds. Hammond & Hammond wasn't the only jeweler in town.

Fact was, though, moxie or no, I never could lie worth a damn.

DECISIONS, DECISIONS

ON the train back home I stared out the window. A hypnotic stream of blurred images jetted past—streetlights; a trash fire in an empty field that belched dark billows of smoke; crowds on piers with cars and boats; a shimmering, colored chaos of envie canopies; gutted, ancient buildings collapsing on themselves in ultra-slo-mo.

At two other local jewelers I'd gotten no farther than I had at Hammond & Hammond. I'd hoped H&H was just being particularly anal, but no one in the jewelry trade deals in cash anymore and my request just made them too suspicious—and I'd come way down on my price, too. So I was stuck with these two incredibly high-quality diamonds in my pocket, more wealth than I'd ever had, that I practically couldn't give away.

Blending with the stark orange city glow to the south, a gentle rose light was spreading above the skyline along the eastern horizon. And Calen wouldn't wait much later than sunrise to send in his odd squad of furniture-moving relatives. Hello, homelessness. I was wealthy as sin, and about to be kicked out on the street.

I couldn't let that happen. Melissa and I were going to have a talk about that stash of hers and whose turn it was to pay the rent.

SERIOUS SHIT, CONTINUED

I opened the door to the apt.

"Melissa," I said, "we have to talk," but by that time my momentum had carried me into the main room, and the words got stuck.

Melissa squatted on the floor of the room with her back to me, in the midst of disaster and debris. Her bag of money was in her lap and the hole by her feet was unboarded. She was talking but I didn't register it. I was too busy taking in the damage.

The bookcases had been knocked over—Melissa's and my books lay scattered across the floor like the corpses of birds: pages plucked loose and strewn like feathers, spines broken. All the posters and photos had been torn down from the walls. Pieces of Melissa's mirror clung in jagged glassicles to its posts, and the pteranodon mobile swung gently to and fro above the air conditioner, smashed to toothpicks.

And my equipment—all my scrounged, inspired brilliance, my cannibalized and jury-rigged hardware. All those years of labor and love. Smashed to jesus. Wiring, screws, bolts, and glass were strewn across the bed, squish-couch, and floor. The blink-beanie had been half flattened, the housing cracked. At least I wouldn't have to worry about Vetch reporting me anymore.

Deep gouges had been slashed in the bed; clumps and strands of cotton stuffing hung out of the gashes like handfuls of entrails. The squish-couch bled liquid in a puddle on the floor. The shelves of computers and amps had been pulled loose and the housings smashed, the delicate innards crushed and battered.

And Tiger—I'd left him under the bed. He lay, broken soldier, beneath a corner of the bookcase— shattered plastic, bent gun, exposed metal guts.

Calen's squad had beat me home.

I crunched across the floor, picked Tiger up, collected his innards, and sat down cradling him in my hands. I brought him to my chest and started to rock him back and forth. Melissa laid a hand on my shoulder. Something ice cold and clammy touched my shoulder blade—I jumped and she jumped. Then I got a good look at her.

"Christ," I said. "What happened to you?"

She raised a baggy full of water and porous lumps of ice to her reddened, swelling cheek. Her other arm was wrapped around the jello-tube, whose black glastic base was cracked. She handed me the jello-phone transceiver. A digital ghost face in the jelly, a simulacrum with hollow silver eyes, stared out at me from under her armpit.

A fucking ghost face. This was getting too jade. I started to hear the screaming again, somewhere, and I was ready to join in at the chorus.

"It's for you, honey," she said, with a strange note in her voice, and handed me the jello-tube. I laid Tiger aside amid the cotton wads and took the jello-tube into my lap. The simulacrum's expression hadn't changed, no big surprise.

"Calen," I said, "don't bother with the ghost face. We know it was you, and our next call is to the Tenants' Legal Co-op. You're dead meat."

"You are mistaken," the ghost face said. "I am not Calen."

It had the typical ghost voice, an androgynous

singsong, a mechanical voice with alien inflections. A client with a thing for privacy.

"Then call back later. I've got a problem on my hands." It was no way to talk to a client, but I was in no mood. I started to hang up.

"I know about the diamonds."

"Excuse me?" My hand hung in midair halfway to the cutoff button.

"I want the envelope you took, or the police will hear about the diamonds you stole."

I recoiled and drew a sharp breath. I looked over my shoulder—Melissa had gone into the kitchen and stood at the refrigerator. Ice cubes rattled against plastic; she was getting more ice for her eye.

"Who are you?" My voice betrayed me—the words came out more air than sound.

"Who I am doesn't matter. Do as I say and you may keep the diamonds; you will hear nothing more from me. Fail to, and the police will receive an anonymous call."

I brushed my hair back. Rachel Karam. It had to be.

"I'm listening," I said after a moment. Melissa came back into the room.

"Here are your instructions. I will give them only once."

"Wait!" I looked around for a computer to enter the instructions to, but everything had been destroyed.

The ghost was already talking. "Take the envelope and a roll of adhesive tape and go to the Manhattan Midtown Scramport."

"Manhattan Midtown Scramport. Envelope and adhesive tape."

"Correct. Be there before midnight. Rent a locker. Lock the envelope inside—"

"Any locker?"

"Any locker. Lock the envelope in the locker and proceed immediately to Grand Central Station with the key. Go to the women's restroom near the Forty-second Street exit."

"Women's restroom, Forty-second Street exit."

"Correct. At the restroom entrance, face your right, go to the last stall on the right-hand side, and tape the key to the trunk of the toilet, at the very back. Make sure nothing is visible from the front."

"Tape the key inconspicuously to the commode in the right-most corner. Right."

"Then leave."

"OK. Then what?"

"If you follow these instructions exactly, that will be all. You'll never hear from me again. Any deviations will result in your exposure and arrest."

I bit my lip to keep from spitting out a retort. Something like, *and how would you explain the will, then, Rachel?*

"You bet," I said. "Whatever you say."

PARANOIA PAYOFF

I was out the door and taking the back stairs three at a time before the ghost face had had time to fade from the jelly. The basement was as dark as a tomb, hot and musty. I flipped on the light, stumbled down the stairs, and made my way through the storage piles and decaying boxes to my cubicle.

Golem and Rachne stood in opposite corners of the nook, untouched. The metal lockbox with my

backup copies of Golem's, Rachne's, and Tiger's
linkware was also untouched, and the tool cabinet
looked exactly the same, too.

Of course, Rachel wouldn't have had to call otherwise. But I wasn't satisfied until I'd dug out a
screwdriver, dragged the tool cabinet out of the way,
unscrewed and removed the drain cover with the
wire hanging from it, and pulled up the baggy tied
to the wire's other end. My heart pounded against
my ribs; I sat down on the concrete floor with the
baggy in my lap and trembled.

Breathe, Ruby, I told myself, pressing a hand
against my rib cage, breathe. Inside the baggy, the
gelpaper envelope with the six remaining stones, the
note, the will, and the cross was still there. Sometimes it pays to be paranoid.

"You want to tell me what's going on?"

I looked up and there stood Melissa at the arch of
my storage cubicle, ice on her eye and hand on her
hip.

I Can Explain
Everything

SHE looked more confused than suspicious. I con-
vinced her we should talk upstairs. I dropped the
baggy into one of my pockets and we went up and
sat on her bed.

"You OK?"

She nodded with a sigh and lowered the baggy of
ice. "Just shook up."

"You're going to get a shiner," I said, and touched
her cheek lightly, inspecting it. The skin was cool,

with beads of water on it from the ice. The bruise was close to the eye and already purpler than mine in spots.

"Yeah." She flashed me a smile that gave me gooseflesh and traced the cut on my own cheek with her fingers. I drew my hand away.

"People are going to wonder why we have matching bruises." A teasing light came into her eyes that made my heart flutter painfully. Then her expression grew sober. "Calen didn't do this. It was a security waldo, and he hasn't got the money to hire one of those."

"Yeah."

"It broke in and started searching the place, smashing things. When I tried to call the cops it knocked me against the wall. It finally left. I don't know what it wanted." She gave me raised eyebrows. "Why would anyone hire a high-tech waldo to break in here, of all places?"

"Mmmm," I said. I didn't want to meet her eyes, so I went into the kitchen and got the broom and dustpan out of the pantry.

"Ruby?"

"Mmm hmm?"

"I get this feeling you know more than you're letting on."

I started sweeping and didn't answer. I could feel her gaze on me.

"I want to know what's going on," she said. "Who was that on the phone, and why did they threaten to call the police? Why did they send a waldo after you? They wanted what's in that baggy you pulled out of the drain, didn't they?"

I kept sweeping.

"Ruby, are you into designers?"

Drugs, she meant. Designer drugs. I stopped sweeping and met her gaze. "Never."

"Then what?"

I gave her a long, hard look. But she'd seen and heard so much already; what else could I do? I sat back down on the bed and pulled the baggy out. On the bed I laid out the cross and chain, the envelope with the Arabic writing, and the note. The diamonds tumbled out last, flashing in the light. Her eyes got wide and her hands went out—she snatched the stones up.

"Diamonds! Christ. Synthetics?"

I shook my head. She poked at them with a finger. "My God, if these are natural diamonds they must be worth millions. Where did you get them?"

When I didn't answer, her eyes got still wider. "You stole them, didn't you? That rich old envie man you found the other night—fuck!" She stood up and started to pace. "That, what's his name—I saw him on the news. Nasser. You stole these from him. Are you *crazy*?"

She yelled this last in my face, shaking her fist which still had the diamonds in it.

"Quiet down," I said, thinking about the neighbors. I might as well have been speaking Arabic.

"The police are going to be all over us! Shit, Ruby, you're out of your mind!" Then she covered her mouth with a gasp and gave me a look that made my skin creep. "Did you kill him for these?"

"Thanks for the vote of confidence."

"Well, what am I supposed to think?"

"Try not jumping to conclusions. If you'll sit down and let me talk I can tell you what happened."

She gave me a look like she didn't want to get too close, but she finally perched on the edge of the bed. I told her the whole story, exactly as it had happened. When I got to the part where Rachel had shown up at the police station Melissa shook the fist full of diamonds at me again.

"Are you trying to tell me that woman would fail to report these as stolen?"

I had this powerful urge to sit on her and wrestle the diamonds out of her hand. Instead I pulled out the note, which she was half sitting on.

"Read this," I said. "Sidra's his son. This was inside the package the old man was trying to deliver when he got shipwrecked."

Her expression grew confused as she read, and then thoughtful. Then an expression came onto her face that made my guts squirm. She laid the note down on my knee and fingered the diamonds in her hand, and then looked up at me with a smile that had relief in it and, well, something calculating.

"She doesn't dare call the police," Melissa said.

"No," I agreed, "she doesn't."

She jumped up with a whoop and clutched the diamonds to her chest. "Then don't you see? We're home free! We're rich, Ruby! It's a miracle. Oh my God, I never thought this could ever happen—"

She went on in that vein. It sounded distressingly familiar. I pulled out the Hammond & Hammond box with the two smallest diamonds and looked at them while she carried on. I put the note, the will, and the cross back into the big, degelled gelpaper envelope and stuck it in my pocket.

The screamer was still going at it, very far away, and I went over to the window and leaned on the sill. Over the tops of the buildings the air shivered and smoked with thrown-off light and heat.

I thought about my dad—a sneak, a thief, someone who terrorized his children and wife, and oh-so-mealy to anyone with a nanospeck of influence. And

Vetch, another fine example of someone who bullied people and stole from them and didn't care who got hurt as long as he made a profit.

The old man, Nasser, he'd been rich, he'd been an envie. Maybe he wasn't the saint they made out on the nets, and maybe he wasn't the world's greatest father, throwing his son out. But he'd tried to help people, he'd tried to do the right thing, it seemed like. And the screamer's voice rolled out so sad, so filled with despair, like he knew no one would hear him, no one would do right by him, no one had to.

That's when I recognized his voice.

"Rest in peace, old man," I whispered. "I understand."

And as the words left my lips, the scream started fading, slowly, the way a siren dies. The silence it left behind soaked right in through my pores and I felt calm for the first time in days—for the first time, in fact, since the skyscraper fiasco.

That more than anything made my mind up for me. I let out a slow, deep breath and turned.

Melissa had fallen silent. She gave me a quizzical look. "You look like you saw a ghost."

"I've been hearing one," I said, and held out my hand for the six diamonds. Her face struggled through several expressions. Then she dropped them into my palm, one by one. I put them in the box with the smallest pair.

"What are you going to do?" she asked. Her voice was very small.

"I just saw on your face what's been in my heart," I said. "And I don't like it." I dropped the box into the pocket with the envelope. "These aren't ours. They belong to Nasser's son—or whoever he left them to in his will. The will—*fuck*." I dug fingers into my hair. "What am I going to do about the will?"

"Listen to me." Melissa took my hands and stared into my eyes. "Listen. They aren't going to miss those diamonds. No one will know. You can't"—I wrenched loose from her and her voice rose in pitch—"you can't just throw them away! *God damn you!*"

"Melissa . . ."

Her face changed again. "I'm sorry, hon. I'm sorry. It's just so much money—I got a little crazy."

She walked in a tight circle like a pent-up animal. Then she came up to me and looked at me with haunted eyes, a travesty of a smile on her lips. She lifted her hands and cupped my jaw.

"It's OK," she said, "I'm OK now," and then she pulled me to her and kissed me, hard and deep, her tongue flicking at my teeth, her hands writhing in my hair.

I pulled away, drew a sharp breath. Tears filled my eyes. That kiss had had knife-blade steel in it.

Her hands dropped to her sides. "I thought you wanted me."

"It doesn't even have to have a penis, does it? Just money."

"Ruby—"

I shook my head, half blind with tears, and stumbled to the door.

"Wait! Where are you going?"

When I looked back she was standing in the midst of the wreckage, her face ashen. "You can't just leave!"

"I have to." I just stood there, though, rooted to the spot, unwilling to leave. Then my glance fell on her bag of money, lying forgotten on the floor. "I've been meaning to tell you, Melissa, it's your turn to pay the rent."

We stood there and stared at each other. Then, not knowing what else to do, I stepped out and closed the door most gently behind me.

JUNKED ON MELISSA

THE jellophone slot swallowed my last five-dollar coin, and after a series of clicks and noises a robotic operator thanked me for using NYNET. Mikey's face appeared on-screen, rubbing the sleep out of his eyes.

"Sorry I woke you."

"Ruby, hey. No prob. What's up? Do I spy e-books and carrels in the background?"

"Yeah. I'm at the New York Public Library."

"You look like hell. Whose fist you run into?"

I made a face. "Who said it was a fist?"

"That bruise sure looks like a set of knuckles to me."

"It's a long story."

"I'll bet. What are you doing at the library?"

"Frying my brains."

"On a controlled substance? At the library? I didn't think you were the type."

"On research. Beat it." This last was to a kid telling me to get off the phone. "Mikey, I need help."

"The way you're saying that it sounds serious."

"It is. I need two favors."

"Go for it, chica."

My guts slithered into a knot. "Can I"—saliva

filled my mouth, and I had to swallow before I continued—"borrow a few hundred dollars? Could you transfer it to my account, um, right now?"

His toothy, overbitten grin came to his lips. There was sympathy in his eyes. I knew the look. *I've been there*, it meant.

"Is that all you need? Hell, I can do that with my eyes closed. Five hundred OK?"

My skin flushed hot—I couldn't figure out whether I was relieved, embarrassed, or irritated by the favor. "I owe you. Five hundred's great. Thanks. I mean it." I clamped teeth together to keep myself from babbling on any further. He gave me a nod.

"You got it. Give me your bank account code."

I transmitted it to him and he put me on hold. I chewed a hangnail while he was gone, till it tore loose and set nerve ends to screaming, and then sucked on my finger with a mental curse.

When he came back he had a toothpick in his mouth. "Mission," he said, "accomplished. How long you need it for? Not that I'm in any big hurry, just want a rough idea."

"I—don't know yet, actually. Hopefully not too long. Which brings me to my second favor."

"Well, go on," he said, grinning encouragement, when I stalled again. "Worst I could do is say no, right?"

"Yeah, OK. I need you to make a phone call."

He seemed surprised. "I must be missing something. You made it sound like something tough."

"It may be tougher than it sounds. The person I want you to call is in a place that may make it hard to get through."

"No problem. I do phone calls for free, for friends. You gonna tell me who to or do I have to guess?"

I gnawed at the flap of throbbing skin that dangled at my nail. "Well, it's a little complicated."

He gave me a penetrating look. "What kind of trouble you in, Ruby?"

" 'mon." The kid tapped my shoulder. "Hurry." His breath was hot on my bare shoulder. He was a skinny kid with high-topped sneakers, baggy shorts, net gloves, earphones. I couldn't even see his eyes through the glaze of dim sparks running through his bug-eye network shades. *Virtu* junkie. No telling how his software was translating me into his private universe.

I opened my mouth to tell him to blow away, to ask him what the hell he needed the phone for, anyhow, hooked into the nets like he was? But something about how he looked stopped me. He was awful young and I guess I felt a little sorry for him; it occurred me that I had been acting like a junkie myself, lately. A Melissa junkie.

I turned back to the phone. "Someone's waiting for the phone, Mikey. I'll be at your place in an hour and a half."

WE PLOT AND PLAN
AS BEST WE CAN

"MR. Nasser isn't in right now," the ghost lips said. "May I take a message?"

"Do y'all know when he'll be back in?"

"I'm sorry; that information isn't in my files. Would you like to leave a message?"

Mikey gave me a questioning look from where he

sat across the room with the jellophone, when I peeked around the corner. I shook my head.

"Nah," Mikey said, "I'll try to reach him later. Thanks very much."

I came around the corner as he broke the connection.

"Just like you predicted," he told me.

"I know he's in there." I glooshed down in the gelbag beside him and worried a fingernail. At this rate, I'd be chewing bone in hours. "The thing is, we have to get to him before midnight. Otherwise that crazy rich woman will send her mechano-goon after me again, and people could get hurt. Like Melissa. Shit shit shit."

"So call her," he said. "Tell her to get out now. She can come over here till y'all get this settled." When I didn't say anything, he added, "What're you waiting for, permission to use the phone?"

I stared at him, feeling bleak. What was I supposed to tell him, that I was terrified of facing her, that she'd probably take a knife to me the next time she saw me?

"You're right." I heaved a sigh and took the phone transceiver he offered. I dialed our home number but the jello-tube stayed blank. After the twelfth ring, I disconnected and gave him an apprehensive look.

"That envie woman don't know you ain't gonna play her game yet," he said. "Melissa's probably just gone out. Or she's asleep or something."

Or, I thought, she's out with Vetch. Or she's killed herself because I was so shitty to her that she's given up hope, or she's gone away forever; she'll never forgive me. . . .

"Not in that mess," I said. "Nobody could sleep there. And Calen's probably already showed up and stolen whatever he could get his hands on that wasn't broken, because she probably didn't pay the rent. Fuck. I shouldn't have left her there alone."

Mikey frowned. He shook his splintered toothpick at me, a mild rebuke. "Look, everybody has fights sometimes. She's a grown woman. She's not gonna shrivel up like a pansy just 'cause you hollered at her a little."

"Yeah, I guess."

"You did the right thing, Ruby, deciding to return the diamonds and will and all. It's not your fault she took it poorly. And if what you said is true, it's high time she paid the rent, anyhow."

"Yeah." But in my thoughts her lips were pressing against mine, her fingers ensnaring themselves in my hair. Desire stirred in me, reptilian and mindless. And I remembered the terrible, ashen look on her face when I'd made that accusation and wanted to curl into a little ball. "Yeah, but I didn't handle it too well."

"I bet it was rough, letting go of all that money."

I nodded and gave him an unhappy look. "I could have used that money. I could have kept her away from sleeping around. She only does it because she needs money."

"That ain't the only reason she does it," Mikey said, softly.

I frowned at him. He didn't know Melissa; I did. And I couldn't help thinking that I'd finally had something that made her want me and I was throwing it away.

"I'll bet I know what you're thinking," Mikey said. "But nothing you do's gonna change her ways. No matter how much money you got or how hard you try. You can plead, you can holler, you can keep paying all the bills. But no matter what you do, she'll keep doing what she does till something scares her bad enough she sees she's got to change. Believe me—I been through it myself."

Then he read the anger in my face. His eyes widened and he rubbed his chin. "Looks like you got some mighty strong feelings for her."

At his words my anger ebbed and my throat tightened. I cleared it and nodded, blinking hard to stop the tears.

"And it's hopeless. She'll never feel the same way I do. I've lost her before I ever had her."

He gnawed his toothpick and looked at me for a long moment. "Yup," he said. "I sorta wondered if it was like that. Hurts like hell, don't it?"

I nodded. His sympathy stripped away all my defenses and I had to just sit and cry for a while. He patted my shoulder, grown awkward, saying, "There now, there there now."

Then I was seeing the old man clutching the envelope—*more precious than diamonds*—and remembering the look on Sidra Nasser's face—*"not in his heart."* I'd done the right thing. The price tag on those diamonds was way too high. And that reminded me of my other problem.

"We're still stuck with how to get his belongings back to him," I finally said, wiping at my eyes and nose with a hanky.

"We could mail the envelope to this Sidra fella," Mikey said. "Or better yet, find a friend of his who could hand-deliver it to him."

"They aren't going to let him get any packages," I said, "No matter who takes it."

His expression was reluctant. "Then I hate to say it, Ruby, but the only other choice is to go to the police and let them handle it."

"Fuck if I'm going to turn myself in! We'll have to think of another way."

"There *is* no other way," he said. He stood up and paced a bit. I could tell he was getting exasperated. "Besides, I can't believe he'd prosecute."

"Yeah, right. This guy's going to let me walk when I just stole several million dollars' worth of diamonds—and his inheritance—off his father's dead body."

He looked defensive. "When you just made sure he got it? Come on. If you hadn't taken that envelope, the police would have returned it to Ms. Karam, unopened, and she would have destroyed it."

That stopped me, for a second. "I hadn't thought of that." Then I shook my head. "The police will talk him into prosecuting. They'll tell him I'm out to blackmail him or something. Cops love to prosecute. It keeps them in business. And envie folk are paranoid of us."

He sat back down next to me, looking deflated. "It ain't just cops. And it ain't just envie folk. You never know who you can trust." He gave his head a rueful shake. "But what else can you do?"

"Wait a minute," I said, straightening slowly as inspiration bloomed inside me. "I have it. We can do a sort of inside-out salvage. We'll take his things straight to him, inside the mansion."

"That's nuts!"

"No it's not. Listen. It'll be the last thing they'd expect. I got mega-data on the house at the library; it's some kind of famous architectural feat and they even have art galleries and give public tours. Not just now, I'm sure, but still, we've got plenty of public-access tapes of the house's interior we can use to navigate with."

"You think he's going to be any less likely to prosecute after you break into his mansion?"

"It's not his mansion; it's Rachel's—and there's no love lost between them. And no. If I hand the diamonds right over to him, he's going to be grateful, not hateful." I paused. "Besides, he's not going to have the chance. I'm going to get in, give him what belongs to him, and go. That'll be the end of it."

"You've got to be kidding."

"I'm serious. I'll send Golem in. He's only going to need a few repairs to be fully functional—"

"And where you gonna get the parts?"

I looked at him. "You're going to have to loan me four of Mash's memory crystals. And his linkware station. We'll install it in your new bird and rig it so I can run Golem from Monster Mash's boards."

"No way." He was shaking his head. "I ain't about to gut my Mash."

"It's the only way."

His jaw set. "No."

I leaned forward, gathered my determination, and met his eyes. "Listen. You know it's the right thing to do. You said so yourself."

"Yeah, so? *You* were the one who made such a mess—" He stopped and looked embarrassed.

"You're right," I said. "I did. I messed up. So don't do it for me. Do it because you know there's a guy in that house who's about to lose his entire inheritance because of someone else's greed. I can reach him—I know I can—but I need help.

"I'll give you back everything I've borrowed once I'm done. I'll replace every piece of Mash's equipment that doesn't make it through this." If I didn't end up on the street, or in jail. "I know it's a big risk. But I can do it. But not without you. You gotta help me. Please."

He gave me a gaunt, worried look. He took my hands in his and stroked the backs of my hands with his thumbs. From the look on his face and the way he avoided my eyes I realized suddenly that he wanted me in the same hopeless way I wanted Melissa. That made me sad.

"Shit," he said. He released my hands and brushed back his mass of loose curls with a sigh. "Shit and shebangles. All right. I must be out of my mind, but I'll help."

"Mikey, thanks."

"Yeah, yeah. OK." A grin struggled back onto his face. "Don't get too mushy, that's all. Us Texan men hate too many emotions getting let out at once."

A NEW LOOK FOR GOLEM

MELISSA must have paid Calen—there was no padlock on the door. She'd even started cleaning up a little before she'd left, which made me feel guilty again for leaving the way I had. We retrieved Golem and my tools from downstairs and collected as much of my other equipment as we could salvage from the mess in the apt.

Mikey and I loaded the stuff into his van and took it all back to his junkyard. In Mikey's storehouse workroom, I plugged all four of Golem's power packs into their fast-chargers while I cut out and removed sections of Golem's dented chassis.

It took a lot of patching to stop the rest of the

hydraulics leaks, and then I rewired and rechipped the damaged circuitry and wiring. With some welds, bolts, and splicing I got his two new arms, the hand-fingered one and the warrior snake arm, secured to the old fittings. The new complement of snake hand attachments fit nicely inside his main chassis compartment along with the rest of his hands and other tools.

I installed the new camera eye onto his vidi platform. The new camera didn't have IR, but it did have a freeze-and-squeeze window option, which could be useful. Then I ran tests on his new arms, and on the two remaining old ones, the telescope and the schwarzenegger. They all seemed functional. The preliminary visuals tests seemed to indicate his new eye was working as expected.

On one of his smaller, underbelly compartments I installed a lock keyed to my voice, and then I rolled up the envelope with the cross and the will and diamonds, stuck them inside, and locked it. I pounded, cut, and welded the damaged sections of chassis to reshape them and give Golem better structural integrity. Then I stood back and surveyed him.

My weld work on the chassis and arms had covered him with multicolored titanium oxides—swirls of cobalt blue, parrot green, yellow and ruby red and purple. A few nicks, scars, and weld burns were all that remained from the accident. Decked out as he was in his shiny party colors, with the two different models of camera mounted on top and his multitude of arms, receptor antennae, wheels, gadgets, and other paraphernalia, he looked like something built by a mechanic with the DTs.

Good old Golem. I tilted the faceplate of my welder's mask up, pulled off my high-temp gloves, flicked away the sweat in my eyes, and then patted him on his psychedelic chassis. You'll do, you old junkbunny.

Where the eye-frying, yellow-and-pink "WAPL News at 11" lettering and logo had been were now blotches of matte-black paint, slowly drying, smelling of turpentine. I tossed my link beanie onto the back seat, along with my tool kit and some spare parts. Nearby, one of the genie cats lying curled at Monster Mash's open hatch gave me a cold cat look and then yawned, flashing yellow teeth; the other, licking its flank with dignified languor, ignored me. Mikey's legs stuck out of the door—the rest of him was under the control panel.

"How you coming?"

I had to repeat the question twice before his muffled voice issued from inside—"A while yet!"

I looked at my watch. It was about two-thirty P.M. Time to do some homework.

SOURCE OF
DIVINE BLESSINGS

Aïn el Baraka, the *Almanet* told me, was a palatial home built up the face of the Palisades, overhanging the Hudson. The Hudson River winds down from the Catskills through the Hudson Highlands, gathering water and silt from mountain tributaries. Somewhere along the way the ocean begins to intermingle with it, and from there on the river makes its slow and salty way southward through the tropical rain forests to the Atlantic Ocean and New York City.

Nasser's mansion was certainly famous enough, but though I'd visited the Palisades as a child and seen pictures of the mansion, I'd never seen the mansion up close and in person—in fact, hadn't even known it was his. According to the syntellect ghost of *Dorian's Almanac of Famous New York Homes*, Aïn el Baraka had been built out from the face of the Palisades, just north of the New York-New Jersey border. It had been "designed and built in 2003 by the famous Moroccan architect Abdallah ibn Ishak under the aegis of the young Youhanna Nasser, then a Harvard lawyer just come into his father's inheritance and a new Coptic sensibility." Whatever that meant.

More importantly, the Almanac ghost had downloaded an hour-long recorded tour of the public areas onto crystal for me, along with a number of three-dimensional floor plans and design details from the Library of Congress. These I promptly dumped to Golem's back-up crystals for later storage in Mash's linkware.

I ran through the tour and then spent another half hour or so studying the house's design and physical features. I could infer some interesting things about their security systems from the uniqueness of the house's design. Aïn el Baraka was more than just a feat of engineering; it was a work of art.

Mikey came in, wiping siloxane grease from his hands. I looked up in time to see the rag he'd wadded and tossed come sailing past me to flutter down over the jello-tube, obscuring the archways, gilt minarets, and shining marble of Nasser's mansion.

"This house is incredible," I said. "They've got art galleries, robotics, passive solar supplemented with a cogen plant—"

"—and security up the yin-yang," he finished,

with a sour grimace. "Those fancy art exhibits and things ain't exactly good news, Ruby."

"We're going to pull it off, Mikey. Have a little faith."

He gave me a look that said, *yeah, sure.* "The linkware is ready. I put the gigacrystals on the worktable."

I snatched up the rag. The numbers floating above the window, Mikey's jelly clock, announced it was 6:06 P.M. Three hours or so to install the gigacrystals and linkware and test Golem's new parts, maybe an hour to get to Aïn el Baraka. That left maybe two hours to break in, find Sidra Nasser, give him his inheritance, talk him into not calling the cops, and get back out before Rachel showed up sometime after midnight. It was going to be close.

"Try Melissa again first," he said, and tossed me the transceiver.

HELLO? HELLO?

SHE answered on the third ring.

"Melissa. Thank God you're home. I—I'm sorry I walked out, I—"

She gave me a remote look that chilled me and I broke off. I was terrified Vetch might be there. I knew that was just obsession but I asked anyhow.

Her arms went across her chest. "I'm alone."

"Are things OK with Calen?" I asked in a wavery, high-pitched voice.

"I took care of it." Her tone was flat.

I wondered if she'd paid him in cash or in some

other way, like she had before I'd moved in. The thought made my stomach flip-flop.

"I know you're still angry with me," I said. "I guess I can understand. Please, just—just listen. OK?"

She folded her arms and looked at me. "I'm listening."

"These people who are after me, they might show up again. I'm worried for you if you stay there."

She shrugged but didn't say anything.

"Mikey Knowles—you know him? He's the guy who owns the junkyard near the wharf—he says you can stay here if you want."

"Why should I?"

Her snide tone pissed me off. "Because your life's in danger and I'm trying to protect you!"

"Oh?"

I took a deep breath, forced my voice down a few notches in pitch and volume. "Melissa, when I don't show up where they told me to be tonight they're going to be angry. I don't want that crazy woman or her security waldo showing up at our place and hurting you again. Or trying to use you against me."

Something changed in her face when I said that. The hungry, pleading look that came onto her face was far worse than her anger had been.

"What are you going to do? You're not going to do something stupid, are you?"

"No I'm not going to do 'something stupid.' I'm going to make things right again. They haven't been right since I took the old man's belongings."

"What does that mean?"

I didn't answer. I felt like her eyes were drilling holes in my forehead. "Rube. Tell me what you're going to do."

I stared back and emptiness spread like novocaine through my chest. But I couldn't lie to her.

"I'm going to take them back to his son. Rachel Nasser is keeping him in her mansion. And I don't want her to be able to use you against me when I break in."

Her eyes widened, and tears gathered in them. She held out her hands. "Please think about this. Think about what you're doing. I'm sorry for what I did, before. Come home and let's talk."

I shook my head slowly, sadly. "My mind is made up."

"Please."

"No. Don't ask again, Liss."

Her expression went remote again. "Then I have nothing more to say to you."

"Just don't stay there. We'll talk about it later."

"Later is *too late!*"

She cut the connection, and her image faded. Mikey was watching from the far side of the jello-tube. I met his eyes.

"I warned her," I said. "I can't tie her up and make her leave."

"Yep," he said.

"I feel like shit."

"That woman knows how to take care of herself. I don't think you got cause to worry."

I gave him a curious look. "You don't like her, do you?"

He pinched his lip, studying me, then shook his head. "Nope, I sure don't."

"You haven't seen her at her best. She's really— very—"

I stopped before his gaze.

"She helped me when I needed her," I finished, lamely.

"Yeah, and you been paying for it ever since." He shook his head. Then the hard expression went away. He gave me a smile.

"Go fix Golem. We're burning daylight."

People Who Live
in Glass Houses

"Where is he now?" Mikey said in my head.

I-Golem looked up through the trees; the "WAPL News at 11" collocopter's blades beat the air somewhere off to my-Golem's left.

I-Golem popped up a vidi menu and made a selection; a three-dimensional grid appeared before my-his vision. I did a triangulation on the sound of the collocopter props. Then, "Got you. You're to my-his northeast, forty-two-point two degrees. I-he am just off the estate maintenance road, nearing the tram at cliffside."

To keep things less distracting for me, Mikey and I were communicating by radio through the linkware. I opened my eyes a crack—Mikey's profile in the pilot's couch beside me was lit up a zombie green from his readouts. The input was distracting, so I closed my eyes again. But in a part of my mind, even through the insulating earphones, the collocopter's blades beat at a different pitch than Golem's audio receptors heard, and sticky, sweaty spots on the copilot couch pressed against the backs of my thighs and my neck and arms.

We'd discovered one of Aïn el Baraka's security measures the hard way: broadband radio signal noise transmitted from radio towers at the cliff face. It made using Golem from a safe distance impossible, and even close up it interfered with the low-energy communications support, like the tracer signal I'd installed on Golem. And Mikey had already boosted the signal to its limit.

The good news was they hadn't detected our intrusion yet. We had ghosted right over the estate's perimeter radar towers in Mikey's stealthy bird, and Mikey had eavesdropped on their transmissions long enough to make sure they hadn't detected us before we dropped Golem off. Then I'd activated the linkware, downloaded my awareness into Golem, and headed for the cliff.

The copter passed overhead. With his IR I-Golem glimpsed two figures behind the bird's darkened windows. I-He dropped forward onto his front set of wheels and rolled on all fours through the underbrush to the edge of a parking lot. At the building on the other side of the lot, beyond a large number of road and air vehicles, several robots or waldos were loading crates from a semivan at the curbside into a tramcar that waited at a platform at the edge of the cliff.

I-Golem reared and swiveled his new eye for a quick, monocular glance at Aïn el Baraka: a white smudge against the maroon and burnt umber of the twilit sky. The mansion seemed to float in midair a hundred feet or so from the cliff face. Light glared from a few dozen of the many windows on its face, and three stout cables of metal braid were slung between the mansion and the cliffside. On this side, the tram cables coiled about a huge, dull-red spool which protruded from the building. The mechanism reminded me of an antique watchworks.

I did a quick scan on my-Golem's transceivers.

The workers' conversation, not to my surprise, didn't broadcast on my-Golem's range of channels.

"Mikey," I transmitted, "see if you can pick up their transmission signals. Are they waldos or robots?"

"Ah. Clever. Give me a minute."

I-Golem dropped again and rolled along the edge of the parking lot at a good clip, keeping a screen of shrubbery and trees between me and the mechanoworkers. They passed out of my-Golem's view behind the building. In a few moments, on the building's other side a horizontal metadiamond strut moved into view, stretching out into the twilight.

I-Golem rolled to a stop. The support strut was thick as a five-hundred-year oak, and clear as ice—so clear I could see in it a miniature, inverted image of the muddy Hudson and the flickering lights on the forested hills of its far bank. The mansion was mostly obscured by the tram building.

"Ruby, you copy?"

"Yeah—go ahead."

"I found the signal. We're in luck. They're bots, and they're controlled from a central, uncoded source. I've recorded the ID imprints of all the units. You ready to go on-line ducky decoy?"

"Ducky decoy it is. Let me-Golem deactivate one of their bots before you switch Golem in, though. We don't want to foul up their tram loader program with one too many inputs."

I-Golem uncoiled his snake arm. It flicked like a real snake crossing sand—so graceful and powerful, so *eager*, somehow, that I wondered whether its programming might somehow be tainted with a killer instinct, whether it might take over and run amok. *Renegade Warrior Arm Wreaks Havoc at Famous Mansion; Five People Killed.*

I-Golem curled the arm up and fitted it with a hole drill and butterfly blades. Then I-he rolled up over the curb and back around to where the robots were loading crates. As one of the squat, rod-and-basket units passed me-Golem, I-he saw that the crate it carried contained a president's ransom in exotic fruit. Grapes and peaches and strawberries, by the bushel. The lettering on the sides looked like Russian; I didn't even want to try to guess how much it had cost to import them.

"Ready, Mikey?"

"Ready."

"Ducky decoy on my signal."

The snake arm lashed out, slammed into the robot's chassis, and drilled through its casing. The robot's talons clacked and flailed wildly—a teeth-jarring burst of broadband radio static screamed in my head. Then Golem's butterfly blades made sparks and scrap metal of the robot's circuitry and it went silent.

I transmitted to Mikey, "Now!" and used the schwarzenegger to wrench Golem's arm loose from the robot unit. Mikey downloaded the tram-loading software and ID imprint into Golem and activated it. Golem slid free of my control—I opened my eyes back in the copter.

That robot was only a machine. I had to tell myself that several times before I stopped feeling like a murderer.

Behind my open eyes, I could half see and hear what Golem was seeing and hearing, as he picked up the crate and bumped over to the tram. He'd refurled the snake arm. Thank goodness. Superimposed over that sight, next to me, Mikey grinned, teeth lit up green. His eyes were hidden behind dark, convex specs filled with dim flickers; earphones covered his ears and a dark worm—his mike—snaked from the phones to his lip. He was checking his readouts. After a moment his voice came, brass-on-rushing water, through my earphones.

"Beautiful. Their control unit only registered a hiccup before Golem took the bot's place. We're in."

I adjusted the mike against my jawline. "Great. Let's find someplace in the forest to put down and I'll go hide the bot before somebody finds it."

"I've got an even better idea." He had a scary grin. Sparks danced on the specs where his eyes should have been. He pointed. "Looky down there. Those vehicles must belong to guests. Look at all those copters—and nobody in sight! We put down in the parking lot, turn the blades off, and stay inside. Perfect place to hide."

"Think it'll work?"

" 'Course it will! What do you say?"

I scanned the parking lot and the tram. He was right. We'd probably be a lot less conspicuous among other helicopters than in the woods. I gave him a nervous smile and a thumbs-up.

"Let me circle around," he said.

I pressed my forehead and hands against the cool glass. Outside, in the falling darkness, the tram and building lay a hundred feet or so below us and several hundred yards to the southeast. Beyond them, out over the river, the mansion rose up on ice shafts that extended from the river below and grew out of the basalt crags of the cliff.

Held aloft like an offering to God, the palace defied gravity and climate. Dark windowpanes slicked, black-ice-like, across the span of frost-marble walls. Spiked bulbs of gold and slopes of ruddy clay tile capped the structure, as if cliff and meadow had been exposed by melting snow. Half-exposed patios, cul-de-sacs, and glass-covered walkways shed soft light. Spotlights at the building's corners hurled shafts of blue-white light at the sky, river, and land.

Massive, airy—a carving of marble, gold, air, and synthetic crystalline rock—it floated, blazing cold light, arrogant and impregnable. I stared at it and a shiver of fear wiggled right up my spine. I almost told Mikey to forget it, then and there.

Lights began to wink on around the parking lot. "We should set down before someone sees us," I said.

THE CROSSING,
ONE

BEYOND the tram's forward window, as the car neared the mansion, two men stood arguing in the unloading dock. The dock was set into an atrium of brass and polished rock: a high ceiling, half an acre of floor space, pillars and plant pots and statuary, all marble and ceramic and brass and slabs of basalt.

The men stood on a strip of carpet that abused several shades of red, which led to the far end of the atrium and from there folded its way up a broad marble staircase. It stopped before a mahogany door you could drive a truck through, which sported a mahogany lion's head with a brass ring in its mouth. Beyond the walls of tinted glass on either side of the door, humans and robots, each of various makes and sizes, moved about on a polished rock floor among more huge vases.

Two monstrous, impassive guards in envie suits

stood at the door. They looked like the ones at the funeral.

When I told Mikey, he looked disturbed. "Ominous."

We were both thinking it: with all the perimeter electronic security to keep people out, why the need to post human guards outside one of the two exit routes—unless you're trying to keep someone *in*?

With a shudder and a deep-throated thud, the tramcar docked. The doors slid open and Golem, following radio instructions from the bot controller, picked up a crate of fresh fruit and debarked the tramcar. My heart gave a wrench when Golem clattered onto the floor of the dock, but the men were too busy arguing to notice a mechanical being, even Golem.

The larger man looked like he was about to melt, in a traditional chef's white uniform with huge rorschach blots of sweat on the back and under the arms. He also wore a white, creased puff of a hat which made me choke on a guffaw, and a juice-stained, full-body apron over the uniform. His bulk and manner made him look more like a longshoreman than a master chef.

Looming over the smaller man, he shook his fists and said with a Brooklyn accent, "The guests have been waiting for over an hour for the compote! The fruits probably all spoiled in this heat. You've got your nerve, holding up my shipment."

"I, too, have been tasked with keeping the guests comfortable, sir," the smaller man replied. He was dressed formally, *au natureil*, a white mandex singlet under translucent black gauze. His hair was waxed into a shimmering white fractal shape—loops within loops within loops and glowing paints in a similar pattern that curlicued over his face and disappeared beneath his singlet, reappearing along his arms and legs. All that glow paint—it made me itch just to look at him.

"The lady authorized the linens to take priority on the last two transports," he said with a dignified air. "You tied up the tram for three transports prior to that, and several guests wanted to freshen up—"

"Where is she? I want her to substantiate this."

"She took one of the yachts into Manhattan half an hour ago."

"Oh?"

"I'm afraid so. You'll simply have to wait till she returns."

I returned to myself. Mikey and I exchanged a look.

"You copy that?"

"Yep. But it's only ten-forty; we still got plenty of time. Get going—we'll get Golem in a side entrance and then I'll guide him to the guest wing."

Golem was heading toward the railing, where stacks of crates and boxes had been piled. I tuned back into him as he was putting the crate down.

"Mikey, disengage—now!"

Golem jerked but I slipped back into control and got myself-him moving again before the break in his programming showed much. With a backward monocular glance at the two men—who were still arguing—I-Golem rolled on past the tram and kept going along the outer walkway.

With nightfall, the walkway had sunken into gloom, lit only by the occasional knob light set along the railing of waist-high, scrolled plaster posts. Golem-high stacks of folded, canvas-wrapped linens partially blocked the path of marbled basalt. That gave me an idea. I-he shook out the FlexBind web and stuffed several packets of towels into it.

The Critic's Choice

MIKEY said the maps were straightforward—"eas-ier'n a stroll through the park"—and I did exactly what he told me: "Go through the second set of glass doors past the indoor patio, down the hall to the end, turn right, then take your first left, then go four doors down and take the fire stairs up to the third floor. . . ."

A pair of servant-type people passed me-Golem in the hall, and they gave me-him some pretty strange looks, but they didn't try to stop me-him or ask any tough questions. After that encounter ended un-eventfully I let myself breathe. I even started to be-lieve I was going to pull this unsalvage off.

Within a few minutes, though, despite the fact that Golem's mechanical presence didn't activate the house lighting system and the rooms and corri-dors were sunk in a sort of warm gloom, things were starting to look familiar.

"Mikey, we've got a problem."

"Yeah, what?"

"How to put this? Next time *I'll* do the map and *you* pilot the beast."

"I ain't got the equipment for it and you know it." Then, as what I said sank in, "You're not there yet?"

"Not even close. I'm in the art gallery."

"The—? You can't be! That's clear over in another section!"

I-Golem gave a nearby bronze bust a monocular

once-over. "Well, Napoleon Bonaparte here begs to differ with you."

"You must not have been following my instructions."

"I did exactly what you said. I even repeated it back."

"I told you exactly what the map said."

While he was talking, distant voices and footfalls floated into Golem's audio receptors. I shushed Mikey. I-Golem popped a grid and swiveled, trying to triangulate, but the sound was bouncing and echoing around too many corners, through the catacomb of rooms. No lights came on, which meant whoever it was was at least a couple of rooms away. The sound soon died away. I relaxed. A little.

"Umm, let's settle the blame later," I transmitted. "Right now we need to get me-Golem out of here."

"I don't know how well we can trust these maps," he said, "but I'll surely try. What room is Golem in? Who's the artist?"

I-Golem dropped onto all four wheels and rolled through a doorway into the nearest room. It was hard to tell in the dimness, but it looked rather like an equipment room.

"That don't seem likely in the middle of the art gallery," Mikey said when I passed this observation along. I enhanced Golem's vision with IR and rolled over to get a closer look at the machinery. The surprise drew a sharp laugh from me, which threw me back to the copter.

"They're artwork!"

Mikey's eyebrows went up.

"John Simon, remember?" I said. "The junk-critter artist. Too schick!"

I tuned back in to Golem, and I-he studied the

Simon "animachines" up close, tried to read a couple of the plaques. I could feel myself grinning. They were all sizes, metals and wire and plastic and lights, from thumb-sized to larger-than-life, made from antique machinery. And most looked realistic but somehow *wrong*: jade, but in a funny, almost animal-like way.

The voices came back then, much closer, and lights flooded the corridor behind me-Golem. I charged Golem's wheels with power and surged around the room, scanning among the sculptures. No place to hide.

". . . personally prefer the classics," a voice was saying. A voice I knew—one that sent several thousand volt-equivalents of adrenaline through my body. "So I haven't been here in a while. But it's one of Uncle Youhanna's most cherished collections."

And then Jehenna followed her words through the archway, and the lights came up. She was followed by Captain Sheila I-Can't-Get-Away-from-You-Anywhere Nanopoulos, good for another near-toxic dose of adrenaline.

Desperation inspired me. I locked Golem into an outlandish pose, full height, arms extended in various contortions, camera eyes askew—which, not coincidentally, gave me a full view of the room—and beat a mental retreat.

Mikey was pulling my hands away from my face. He had a toothpick between his lips and worry in his eyes. "You're about two shades paler than a white woman ought to be able to get."

"Holy fuck," I said. It was all I could manage. I was trembling.

"I hear the voices. Who is it? Where's Golem?"

"I'll explain later." I made a fist of my resolve and plugged back in.

They were staring right at me-Golem.

"I don't know," Jehenna was saying. "I've never seen it before. I thought it moved."

"Must have been the lighting." A pause. "It doesn't have a plaque. Interesting. It looks familiar." Nanopoulos studied me-Golem, chin in hand, with a narrow, thoughtful look that drenched me in icy, sweaty dread. "I've seen this thing somewhere before."

"Oh? Where?"

I thought about having Golem take her and Jehenna out with the snake arm. Maybe I could still find Sidra before they could stop me-Golem. The only thing that stopped me was a fear I'd accidentally kill her. That'd be good for a trip off the planet—the hard way.

Nanopoulos said, slowly, "The Guggenheim, maybe. Or was it the Met? I've been to both museums recently, but I can't remember now which one."

"Maybe it was just a similar piece."

"I can't imagine Simon doing two alike."

"This one is certainly unique." Jehenna peered at me-Golem with a rather dubious expression. She waved a hand at Golem's chassis. "It's certainly eye-catching, what he did with the rainbow coloring on the metal." A pause. "I can't decide if I like it."

"I do. This sculpture is quintessential Simon."

They studied me-Golem until I started to squirm in the copilot's seat.

"I wonder what the linens signify?" Jehenna asked.

"Maybe servitude."

"I'd sure hate to have a bot like that waiting on *me*. It would give me nightmares."

They both laughed and moved on to study a couple of the other sculptures. I took the opportunity to transmit a quick update to Mikey on who they were.

"Holy fuck is right," he said.

Nanopoulos had changed the subject.

". . . attending the wake? Traditionally it's supposed to last three days, right?"

"That's right. Attendance is down from yesterday. We have about four hundred local people attending tonight's gathering. And about a hundred additional overnight guests, I think." After a pause she said, "We really appreciate all you've done, Captain."

"After all he did for my dad it was the least I could do." A pause. "It's hard to believe he's gone. When I was little I thought of him as immortal—he had such presence, such power to persuade."

"Yes. I keep thinking I hear his voice. I keep expecting to turn a corner and find him there."

"Rachel seems to be taking it hard."

Jehenna nodded. "She lost him so suddenly."

"This sort of thing never seems fair to me. He was in excellent health. If only that salvage woman had come along sooner maybe he'd still be alive. Or if he'd postponed his trip. What was he doing out in a hypercat right before a hurricane, anyway?"

"I guess we'll never know," Jehenna said.

Mikey snorted. My sentiments, exactly.

Nanopoulos asked Jehenna, "Where is Rachel now?"

"Resting, I think."

"Good. I'm sure she needs it."

A series of high-pitched, staccato beeps issued from somewhere in the vicinity of Jehenna. She pulled a kelly out of her pocket and when she activated it a hologram appeared in her hand—an Egyptian-looking man in a security uniform. A glint of silver on his crown told me he was a beanhead.

"We've found a bot destroyed at the tram house, cliffside," he said. "Someone must have penetrated the maintenance software and substituted a waldo for the destroyed unit. They probably came across with a load and are in the house now."

"Shit," I said. I opened my eyes and looked over at Mikey.

"For crying out loud," he said. "We're fucked."

I touched my lips for silence and retuned into Golem.

Nanopoulos had said something I'd missed. Jehenna looked irritated. "News media, most likely. We had trouble with them yesterday."

"I can summon a couple of squad units."

"No. I don't want to disrupt the wake and we have plenty of internal security. Ahmed, have Housekeeping switch over to hard wiring on all the bots and waldos, notify the guests that radio communications are going to be hampered, and then drop a white-noise sheet over the house. That should disrupt their transmissions long enough for us to find the intruder. Focus the search in guest and party areas. They're probably looking for unauthorized footage of the wake."

"There must be a signal booster on the estate—maybe they bribed one of the guests to drop it on the grounds somewhere like yesterday. Radar hasn't detected anything bigger than an owl all evening, and they couldn't be getting through the perimeter security with an unboosted signal."

The frown on Jehenna's face deepened. "If that's so, you people in Security haven't been doing your job. All guests were to be screened electronically before entering the grounds."

"I'll find out who or what was responsible for the error."

"Do that."

"Do you want me to use Tiny Tim, as well?"

"No. Leave him in storage for now. Give me regular updates on your progress."

I could feel Mikey's gaze on me, and returned to the copter. He flicked his chewed-up toothpick over his shoulder. I gave him a look. You know—a *look*. "You heard?"

"I heard," he said.

"We've maybe got half an hour."

"Huh."

"So what do you think?"

"Huh." His brow piled into a stack of *m*'s. He reached into his flight jacket, pulled out a small gold case, extracted a new toothpick, and stuck it between his teeth. Then he skull-grinned me.

"I think you'd better make it snappy," he said.

ROOM SERVICE,
ONE

KNOCK knock.

"Who is it?"

"Room service, ma'am. May I offer fresh towels?"

The door slid open, and beyond it a woman walked, bare buttocks receding, toward the bathroom—a towel-draped hand rubbing a mess of wet hair with alarming vigor. She waved a vague hand toward the mattress piled high with tangled sheets in the alcove.

"Throw them on the bed, would you?"

A multilevel heat, light, and sound scan. No Sidra.

Room Service,
Two

Knock knock.
  A pause. No answer.
  Knock knock.
  Still no answer.
  KNOCK KNOCK.
  Still no answer.
  I-Golem stood a long moment, scanning for sounds at the door. No sound inside, not even breathing; no Sidra.

Room Service,
Three

See Room Service, Two.

Room Service,
Four

See Room Service, Three.

ROOM SERVICE,
FIVE

KNOCK knock.

Beyond the flying-open door stood a large man with a totally bald head shaped like a ballistic missile. The glower melted to a look of alarm or perhaps disbelief when his gaze focused on me-Golem, and curdled into a half-perplexed, half-angry frown.

The upper half of an anorexic woman appeared from behind him, holding her hair with one hand, teeth and fingers of the other hand prying apart the jaws of a clip. The hair cascaded out, waterfall-like, mostly from a central point, and lit up in a shifting array of colors like backlit fiber-optic cables. Her diaphanous gown, briefly glimpsed, flashed phosphorescent fireworks in tandem with her hair.

A muffled shriek issued from her when she saw me-Golem—mouth and eyes flew open—the clip tumbled to the ivory-colored carpeting.

"What is *that*?"

"No cause for alarm, ma'am, sir. Housekeeping service."

"They finally brought the bedclothes. It's about damn time. They didn't even give us a balcony room, and now this."

"Please don't use curse words, Frank."

"I don't care. It's been over an hour. Hurry up about it. What are you doing? I don't believe this. You moronic machine! We didn't order towels. We need sheets. Damned idiot. Go back and get *sheets*. King-sized sheets. And pillowcases. You get me?"

"Yes, sir. King-sized sheets and pillowcases. I shall return *post haste*, sir."

"Please don't curse, Frank."

"I don't care, damn it. Fool machine." From beyond the shutting door: "What have you done to your *hair*?"

ROOM SERVICE, SIX

SEE Room Service, Four.

ROOM SERVICE, SEVEN

KNOCK knock.

After a pause, a man's voice: "Who's there?"

"Room service."

"I didn't call room service."

Knock knock.

"Who's there?"

"Room service, sir. Fresh towels."

"I said I don't want room service. Beat it."

Knock knock.

Another pause. The door slid open and a young man wearing a scowl and a Japanese-style robe stood on the other side. A white man. His erection, which made the cloth poke out, was slowly deflating. A swift multilevel scan of the room revealed a young woman in the bed with sheets pulled up to her chin. No Sidra.

"Sorry, sir. Wrong room."

His face contorted. "You—" he sputtered, and slammed the door.

ROOM SERVICE, EIGHT

KNOCK knock.

"Who's there?"

"Room service, sir. Fresh towels."

"Fresh towels? That would be just the thing." A pause. "Your voice sounds mechanical."

"I'm a robot, sir. Housekeeping bot. Fresh towels?"

"Yes, thanks; bring them right in."

I-Golem stared at the closed door for a minute, and I could feel myself frowning.

"What is it?" Mikey transmitted.

"Strange. Hang on."

"Sir," I-Golem said, "the door is closed. My programming requires the door to open before I enter."

"Ah. That is a problem." The man's voice sounded strained, artificially cheerful. "You see, I think the door is jammed. Er, do you have the equipment to open it?"

My heart started to flutter in my chest like a trapped bird. "This is it," I told Mikey. "I recognize his voice. They've locked him in from the outside."

"I believe I have the right equipment," I-Golem said. "Step back, please."

I-he extended his schwarzenegger arm, gripped the

door handle, tightened the grasp till the handle dented, locked his wheels, and *pulled*.

Nothing happened for a second. Then, with a grinding scream and a snap, the lock mechanism broke and the door slid open.

Sidra stood on the far side, looking the way I remembered him—rather tall and lean and athletic looking, like a runner, with black skin and a shaven head, prominent cheekbones, a reticent chin, aquiline nose, and hazel eyes hollowed and darkened. He wore his red and yellow novitiate robes, belted with cloth at the waist, and sandals.

Sidra looked from me-Golem to the shorn handle in Golem's hand, and surprise crossed his face. Then he stuck his head out the door and looked both ways. He passed me-Golem and started down the corridor.

"Ack," I said.

"It's him," I transmitted, executing a hurried K-turn.

"Sidra?" Mikey's voice sounded incredulous.

"Wait," I-Golem called, speeding after Sidra. "Wait!"

Over his shoulder he threw me-Golem a look of dismay. "I don't need towels. I've changed my mind. Go away."

At an intersection with another corridor he slammed into a man carrying luggage. They both stumbled back.

"Excuse me," he gasped, "may I borrow your kelly?"

The man shook his head, opened his mouth.

"A netphone?" Sidra rushed on.

The man shook his head again and squeezed out a "Sorry, I—" but by that time Sidra was gone.

Both the man and the woman beside him moved

back against the wall as I-Golem sped past them, gearing down for the corner, mechanism grinding. Two children—a girl about ten and a boy about five—came around the corner, blocking my-Golem's way. I-he screeched to a halt, nearly tipped over.

A look of delight burst onto the girl's face. "Freaking wonky. Daddy, I want one!"

The boy took one look at me-Golem and started to scream.

"Wait!" I-Golem dodged around the kids as Sidra disappeared into a stairwell down the hall.

TRACKING SIDRA

I-GOLEM looked down the stairwell, and then up. I-he strained his audio-receptors. Faint echoes above; ditto below.

"They've got the house systems tied up," I transmitted. "That's why he's looking to borrow someone's personal comm system. Maybe he's trying to call the police."

"And report his stepmother for kidnapping? Come on."

"Yeah, well," I started, but he interrupted, sarcastic.

"Yeah, well, what? Who'd believe him? He's some disinherited crackpot from a mother-earth cult and this Karam woman is now one of the wealthiest women in the western hemisphere."

"It's not right."

"No, but it's life. I bet he's trying to get hold of his cult buddies, tell them what's happened, get help that way. Them cultists, they don't trust the police any more than you do, chica. They don't trust nobody."

That pissed me off, but I didn't say anything because he was right.

"Looky here—I'll give you odds he's just trying to get out. And there are only two places he can go to get away. Either the tram or the glass elevator."

"You can see the tram," I transmitted, "so we have one route covered. I guess that means I-Golem'll cover the elevator. But he could get on at any floor and be down to the river in no time. How'm I going to know?"

"It ain't necessarily gonna be that easy for him."

"Huh? I've passed at least four elevators since I entered the building."

"That glass elevator that goes down to the river docks ain't connected to the internal house transport system. There's only two entries."

"Oh yeah?"

"Yeah. I'm looking at the map right now. There's an entry at the inner atrium in the back of the house, behind the hanging gardens, and the same location down in back of the recreation center."

"So he'd have to get on the glass elevator in the first-floor atrium or at the bottom of the hanging gardens behind the rec area," I said. "I'll give you odds they have both entrances to the river elevator under watch, just like they do the tram."

"Seems likely. Now, there is a chance he could have gone up the stairwell instead of down. Do you think he's got any reason to go up? Like to the roof?"

"Nope."

"That's what I figure, too. According to my map the stairwell you're in goes straight down to the pool. So," he said, "*I'll* give *you* odds he took the stairs down to the rec area and is trying to figure out how to get past the guards down there."

I-Golem tipped back and started bumping down the steps, clinging to the rails with the finger-hander and the telescoper. "I sure hope so. Whiteout's coming; we can't afford to be wrong."

SIDRA EXPERIENCES
DISBELIEF

MIKEY'S hunch was good. Sidra stood behind a planter filled with chrysanthemums and marigolds, his back to me-Golem, straining to see past the plants. A clot of children ran past behind him, shouting. Sidra jumped, alarmed.

On the other side of the planter, water gurgled in the Jacuzzi, in which several nude adults sat, sniffing and laughing and rubbing at their eyes from what must have been a sinus-searing dose of chlorine. And from where I-Golem stood, looking through the glass stairwell door, a woman dressed in the house security uniform was visible standing, arms folded, next to the bar.

The planter where Sidra hid lined a walkway set in glazed porcelain that curved around past the pool and the badminton court. The pool was filled with rafts of candles set amid lilies, white roses, and pale, spotted orchids. Beyond the mesh that surrounded the badminton court, behind a glass wall, were woven rafters of tropical greenery and lush flowers— the hanging gardens. Beyond *that* should be the elevator to the river, if memory served me. Throughout the rec area, metadiamond struts supported the mass of the mansion overhead and played with the light of the torches set around the pool.

Robotic servers and maîtres d'hôtel carried trays of food and drink and wandered among the few guests lounging in the poolside chaises or standing at the bar. An oversized acoustic guitar skated on its stilts from group to group, tickling its wire-strung belly with spidery hands. Classical music spilled out from beneath its fingers.

"Not as many people as I expected," I transmitted.

"I bet there's more inside where it's cooler," Mikey said.

I-Golem used his zoom and saw that the servers and maîtres d' all had cords leading from their backs to a grid of nearly invisible wires that ran overhead. Perhaps twenty minutes had passed since Jehenna had ordered the white-noise sheet.

Whiteout, any minute now. I had a sudden urge to bolt.

Footsteps hit the stairs behind me-Golem. I-he rolled out of the stairwell and held the door for a nude young man followed by a nearly nude woman. Sidra heard them and moved forward, grabbing the woman's arm. His voice was urgent and low.

"May I borrow your kelly?"

She smiled apologetically, motioned at herself. She was dressed only in a gauze wrap, clearly without pockets.

"Haven't got it with me. Sorry."

Sidra's fist punched the air in a motion of frustration—then he spun with a muffled yell when I-Golem tapped him. Dismay settled onto his face again when he recognized me-him.

"Look. Go away. *Stop following me.*"

I lowered Golem's speaker volume and dropped to all four wheels. "Sidra Nasser, I'm not a robot. My name is Ruby and this is my waldo Golem. I'm here to deliver a message from your father."

His face went slack with shock. "What?"

"Can we talk someplace more private?" I-Golem asked, as yet another person strolled past. "It's important and we don't have much time."

"What sort of sick joke is this? My father is dead. Who are you?"

"I told you. I'm Ruby. Ruby Kubick. And I know your father's dead. I was there when he died."

Sudden recognition pushed the skepticism off his face.

"Ruby Kubick," he repeated. "The woman who . . ." His voice tapered away and he swallowed. "He . . . he gave you a message for me?"

"Well, sort of. Look, there has to be a better place to discuss this."

He studied me-Golem, then drew a breath. "Follow me."

Sidra led me-Golem through a corridor, around to one of the outer walkways that faced the cliffs.

"Lights down," he commanded, and as the globes dimmed he turned to face me-Golem again. His face was shadowed. By this time I-Golem had keyed open the secret compartment. I-he pulled out the gelpaper envelope and extended it.

"Your father was on his way to have this delivered to you when his hypercat capsized," I-Golem said.

Sidra took the envelope, read his name on the front, frowned. He pulled out the note and the will. His face didn't change expression as he read the note. Then he looked up at me-Golem.

"He didn't reinherit me. I was there for the reading."

"They read the wrong will. The old one."

He looked at the note, turned it over, examined the smaller, ribboned envelope with the Arabic writing on it. Then he looked up at me-Golem again. His hands were trembling and the same dreadful look came onto his face that had appeared at the funeral.

"I don't know who you are or what you think you're doing with *this*," giving the note a shake, "but I'll bet I can guess."

"I'll bet you can't."

"Oh, I think I can. I'll bet you think you're clever. I'll bet you think you're the first person to come up with the idea of taking advantage of my relationship with my father, and you've come up with this great scam to take me for all I'm worth, or to get to his fortune through me.

"Well, whoever you are hiding behind that machine, I have news for you. I've seen it all. You have no idea how many times. And I'll bet you think you're safe hiding behind that machine, but if I ever find out who you really are—"

"Whoa," I-Golem said, "wait! You've got it wrong. Listen to me. This is real."

"I'll take that chance." He hurled the two envelopes and note at me-Golem and stalked off.

The envelopes struck Golem's chassis—I-he grabbed at them. The Coptic cross and chain slithered out of the gelpaper envelope and struck the pavement. The note fluttered away, caught by the breeze, and the diamonds went skittering across the stones, hurling light flecks. By the time I-Golem had collected the items and stuffed them back into the gelpaper envelope, Sidra was long gone.

"Hoo-ee," Mikey said in my head. "Got himself an attitude."

I-Golem headed back toward the pool, feeling half angry and half freaked, making my head spin. I couldn't think too clearly.

Mikey said, "I say fuck it. It ain't your problem if he turned down his inheritance."

"Guess he gets a lot of assholes bothering him or something."

"Forget about him! They're gonna drop the noise sheet any minute."

Mikey's reminder shook me loose of my shock. Whatever his reasons were, he was acting like an asshole, and I wasn't about to sacrifice Golem for another chance to argue with him about it.

"Yeah. You're right."

"Send Golem down by the river elevator. Even if they got guards there, nobody's going to stop Golem. They'll think it's part of his programming."

"OK. You're right."

"And stop worrying, Ruby. You done all you could do."

"I wonder if he made it out," I said.

"Probably not. Security's too tight."

After a second, when I didn't say anything, Mikey added, "He'll be all right. He's not breaking any laws and they can't keep him locked up forever. But if you don't get Golem's big tin-can ass out of there, they're going to find him and haul you to jail for trespassing. Or worse."

I-Golem locked the envelope away again—if I lost Golem to a whiteout, I didn't want the envelope in plain sight—and then rolled along past the partyers at the pool, past the badminton court. I-Golem went through a set of climate-lock glass doors and entered the hanging gardens.

Beside me-Golem was an ebony and brass railing, and the floor on the other side of the railing was made of glass. A sign made of pale-pink neon set into the ebony said DANGER! DO NOT CLIMB OVER RAILING OR STEP ON METAGLASS! Beneath the metaglass floor, the lighted glass elevator shaft rose through the darkness from the lighted boat dock at the river's edge far below.

I-Golem rolled over to the railing and looked up. Lit by bars and globes, a forest of leaves, runners, ferns, rafters, and vines hung suspended—great baskets and twined branches in thatched nets and platforms—emerald, African blue-greens, dark and light and gold and cool greens—and splashes and cascades of flowers weaving through in red, lavender, white, butter-gold, pink, and blue. The support struts, crystalline tree trunks, rose among them and along the sides.

The hanging plants were spread just evenly enough, kept trimmed just so, that they cast green shadows all the way from the metaglass ceiling, beyond which stars were visible nine floors up. Birds chirped and leaves twitched overhead in engineered breezes. I wondered if those were real birds, and if so, how they kept the bird shit off the glass floor and the balconies.

On this floor and the floor above, a walkway surrounded the garden on all sides. Higher up, semicircular balconies surrounded the garden on all but one side. That side was a sheer, nine-story wall of metaglass.

I was far enough back to see, unobstructed by the first-floor balcony, the starlit night sky through the leaves and the metaglass wall. To the west, a waxing moon hung over the dark hills. Sheet lightning ionized the sky in the south. The beauty of the gar-

dens and the glass and the night beyond caught me
so by surprise that it froze my breath in my chest,
made my nose sting and my eyes tear.

There are a lot of things I've been missing, I realized, and wished suddenly I could stand in that
garden myself. I wanted to smell the plants and dirt
and flowers, touch the handrail, pick up a leaf, instead of seeing it all at a remove.

Mikey coughed. The air in my nostrils was hot
and close, smelling of sweat-heated vinyl and old
leather: Mikey's Army flight jacket.

"What's happening?" he transmitted.

I forced myself to concentrate. "Storm's moving
in."

"Tell me about it." He sounded tense.

I-Golem rolled around toward the elevator. A
small tiled vestibule lay before me-him, and there
was the river elevator entry, in brass, glass, ebony,
and black enamel. No elevator car was inside. To
either side of the elevator was metaglass, and beyond, the hills.

Two beefnecks stood in front of the elevator,
blocking Sidra's way.

"Just what the hell is going on here?" Sidra demanded. "Who told you to restrict my passage?"

"I'm sorry, sir, but you'll have to wait to speak to
Ms. Karam," one of them said. Sidra looked at the
guard, opened his mouth, closed it. Then he tried to
shove past the guard and push the elevator button.

The guard grabbed his arm, twisted it behind him,
and pinned him against the elevator shaft wall.
Sidra, cheek pressed to the chrome, bucked and
struggled; then the guard said something in his ear
that made him go still.

"Aw, shit," I said. Mikey said something but I
didn't hear it. I-Golem reared onto his hind wheels,

whipped out all his arms, and moved forward: an eight-foot, one-thousand-pound mechanical monster with nasty-looking appendages bristling like something out of a surgical nightmare.

"Let him go," I-Golem boomed at his highest volume. The guards spun, gaped at me-Golem. The one holding Sidra yanked him aside; the other pulled out a gun.

"Not that—you'll draw the guests," the one holding Sidra snapped. "Call Ahmed."

They backed along the walkway, one guard holding Sidra in a half-nelson, who was kicking and twisting in grim silence, the other pointing the gun at me-Golem and whispering into his kelly.

"Help!" I-Golem yelled at the top of his voice, waving his arms. "Fire! Murder! Rape! Help, someone! Come quick!"

Sidra twisted far enough to knee his guard in the balls. The man doubled over with a grunt—Sidra double-fisted him in the face and he went over backwards in an arc. For a priest, he was mean with a punch. Sidra ran toward me-Golem and the other guard.

Footsteps slapped the pavement behind me-Golem, nearing. I-He rushed the man with the gun—ignoring the slug that ricocheted off Golem's chassis—whipped out the snake arm, and hugged the guard, lifting him off his feet. With the schwarzenegger I-he took the gun away. The guard's face started to turn red; maybe I-Golem was squeezing too hard.

I-Golem dropped him and handed the gun to the first guest who came running up. Sidra passed me. Several people were rushing up behind; others peered over the railings from the balconies overhead.

"Don't let them get away," I-Golem boomed. The guest with the gun winced and I lowered the volume. "They're criminals."

He pointed the gun uncertainly at the two security guards. "Aren't these men house security?" he asked.

"What's going on?" someone asked. Other voices rose.

"You're in a lot of trouble," the guard I-Golem had hugged said. "I'm going to sue. You broke a rib."

"Then you'd better sit still," I-Golem advised, "or you'll pierce a lung."

Sidra went up to the guest with the gun. "Give me your kelly. Hurry."

The guest dug into a pocket with his free hand, pulled out a hand-sized kelly. Sidra snatched it from the man's hand, typed in a number. After a pause, a hologram of a Forest Veils priest appeared in the palm of Sidra's hand.

"Would someone like to tell me what's going on?" the guest with the gun asked.

"It's kind of a long story," I-Golem told him.

"Cousin Nasser!" the hologrammatic priest said. "When we heard nothing more we began to grow concerned."

"With good reason. They've been holding me against my will—"

But the hologram turned to milk, as signal noise rose to a gravel avalanche in my head and Sidra shouted, "No!"

"Lock down, Ruby!" Mikey was shouting in my ear. He was shaking me by the arm. "Lock Golem down!"

I transmitted the locking command, but couldn't tell if Golem got the signal in time. Everything whited out.

A Parting of Ways,
Take One

I came to in the copter, one hand holding the disengaged beanlink connector wires and the other on
the door handle. Mikey had both hands on my right
wrist and hand, trying to pry my fingers loose from
the handle.

"Easy," he said, holding me down. "Easy."

I fought him. "Golem's in there!"

"You gotta wait. Security's all over."

He was right. Outside the smoked window, beyond the other copters, cars, and buses in the
mercury-lighted parking lot, a group of envie-suited
figures was milling around. Security.

I went cold and started to shake—stopped fighting
Mikey's hold. I'd nearly burst out into their waiting
arms.

Mikey saw my expression and let me go. He had
binocs around his neck now and a netglove on his
right hand. His lip and forehead were collecting
beads of water. He gave my arm a squeeze. He really
stunk—serious BO. Or maybe it was me.

"They been there a while. They're searching the
woods for electronics. I turned off the engine so they
wouldn't hear it running and come investigate."

The temp was probably not much hotter than
110 degrees, uncomfortable but not deadly. A gust
of wind made the copter shudder and lightning
traced the sky to the south.

I took some deep breaths to calm myself and sat
forward, unpeeling my back from the seat with a

velcro noise. My fingers trailed over my dripping hair, the warm metal jack at my crown.

"Eventually they're going to do the parking lot," I said.

"They've found their intruder. There's no need."

Even as he spoke, the suited figures were beginning to gather at the tram. Others came out from the woods.

I felt sick. I covered my face. "Shit."

"Ruby." Mikey took my hands. "Golem's a goner and so's the will and the diamonds. A storm's coming in. We gotta get out of here. You gave it your best shot. Comes a time to cut the losses and let go."

"No." I started shaking my head. "No."

"Ruby—"

"I can't stop now. I won't leave Golem in there. I'm not giving up."

"It's a machine, damn it. A machine!"

"*No!*"

I threw off my belt straps, scrambled into the back seat, grabbed my linkware beanie.

The engines started up. I turned. Mikey's jaw had set.

"We're taking off, chica," he said. "Sit down."

I showed him the beanie. "This'll work if I can get close enough. I'm going in."

I shoved open the door that faced away from the tram building, fell out, and slammed it shut. The guards had seen the blades start up and one or two were coming toward it, breaking into a run. I dove for cover beneath a collolimousine at the edge of the parking lot—barked my forearm, got a faceful of grime, and took dirt up the nose.

"*Damn* you, Ruby!" Mikey said in my ear. I'd left the earphones and mike on. The blades were beating faster. I spat dirt out, wiped my mouth.

"Go!" I said. "Watch the roof. Wait across the river."

One of the guards was almost to the copter.

"On the roof, then. Damn you."

The copter lurched into the air and shrank upward toward the gathering storm clouds.

Staying low, I scrambled into the dark woods and stumbled around to the far south side of the building, away from the security guards. The wind, potent with the smells of mildew, leaves, and wood turpentine, fought me. My eyes teared. When I reached the building wall, the security people had gathered in a knot near the tram, talking. The wind carried the individual words away.

The riverward side of the building was well lit; I crouched in the shadow at its southern edge, near the horizontal support strut. The strut came out a good eight or ten meters below the edge of the cliff. In the dimness I could make out a short, rocky slope down to the cliff's edge.

The tram building's face was bare and flooded with lights. There was no way to get to the roof of the building, to climb onto the tramcar roof, without being seen. So I decided to go across on the support strut.

THE CROSSING,
TWO

THE leather sandals were no good for climbing but they were all I had. I tied the layers of my gauze clothing in knots at the elbows, waist, and ankles. The beanie I put on, and deactivated it to shut out the brain-shredding white noise. The headphone-mike set I tucked into my belt.

I left the shadows, sprinted for the cliff, and slid down the hill on a slide of rocks, praying no one would look my way during those few seconds. The wind hid the sound of rocks tumbling that my heels and buttocks loosened. I threw my weight flat and slowed the slide, digging my hands and heels in. At the cliff edge I looked down.

It wasn't quite as bad as I'd feared; there were outcroppings and ridges I could use, and, as my eyes became adjusted, with the light from the house and the moonlight there was enough to see by. I rolled over onto my belly, scooted over the edge, and clung to grass while my toes sought the first rock. Found it—and I was over the side.

Crouch. Drop. Scoot. Grasp, dig, slip, grab, grope, drop, cling. I looked down, panting, and the strut was just below. I was covered with scrapes and bruises. It cuts down on wear and tear in a big way, using a waldo for this sort of thing. And besides, Golem fixes up a lot easier than I do.

One last scoot and drop and my heel struck the strut. I crouched, hands on the cool, curved glass for balance. The house was a hundred feet away. And the river almost five hundred down. Given my druthers, I preferred the house. I turned, stood, put my arms out, and started to walk.

The first few steps were surprisingly easy. Then a gust of wind hit me—the leather of my sandal slipped across the glass. I cartwheeled my arms, went to my knees, hard, and tightened all my muscles to steady myself. Then I spent a few seconds trembling and trying not to throw up.

After that, I crept along on my knees. It was a long crawl and my knees kept slipping and banging on the low-friction surface; by the end of it the nerve endings in my knees and palms were screaming.

The strut entered the structure about a story below the rec area. There was only one way up: stout cables of wire braid fanned out and up from a piton in the strut to various locations along the wall, just beneath the rec area wall. The shortest of them was maybe five meters long.

I rested for a minute, sitting with my legs wrapped around the piton, and then tested the wire. Not a bit slippery, and the braiding gave it a good grip.

I stood. I was so scared my body felt like all the blood had drained away. I looked down between my feet and then up at the house.

"Here goes," I told myself. "I'm not ready to die yet, so don't fall."

Then I got a good hold, wrapped my legs around the cable, and started to shimmy backwards up the wire using hands and feet, dangling like an orangutan.

It really wasn't all that far and the slope wasn't too steep. By hanging my head back and looking upside down I could see my destination: a row of decorative marble braces shaped like numeral 6s jutted out along the wall beneath the balcony, with winged angel busts on top of them. As I shimmied close, I let go with my legs, turned around so I dangled facing the house, and swung my legs out and up to catch hold of the lower curve of one such brace with my feet.

Then I reached up with a hand and grabbed hold of the marble angle. I nearly slipped and fell but got an arm wedged between the angel's wing and its neck. With a last burst of adrenaline, liberally mixed with sheer panic, I pulled myself up onto the brace, scrambled over the top of the carving, and got up over the wall. I landed on the slate walkway—and the lights came up.

With my wrap and baggy pants in filthy tatters from the climb, the last thing I needed was to be seen. Of course, all anyone had to do was walk past, and they'd collapse from anoxia. I *really* stank.

I ordered the lights dimmed and bent over and practiced my breathing till my vision cleared and the nausea ebbed. Then I straightened, untied the knots from my ruined clothes, and looked around. I stood near where Sidra had thrown the envelope in my-Golem's face. At a run, I headed around the south end of the walkway toward the pool.

At the corner where the basalt tiles met porcelain, I stopped. Only five or six guests were left at the pool, three of them in the Jacuzzi and a couple of others kicking their feet in the water at the pool's edge, making the candle-and-flower rafts bob up and down. Beyond, I caught a glimpse of Golem and some people inside the gardens.

I sat down cross-legged on the basalt and turned on the beanie linkware. The programming dampened the signal noise to a bearable level—and I downloaded into Golem.

Visuals were low-res and snowy, but steady. I-he

was still at the elevator; a woman and three men, all house security, were heaving and shoving at me-Golem, their heads bobbing around at a level even with the top of his chassis. So—the lock command had reached him after all.

Jehenna and Captain Nanopoulos were there. Sidra was nowhere to be seen. Neither were the two security guards who'd tried to stop him.

Nanopoulos watched them try to move me-Golem. She said something over her shoulder to Jehenna, seeming puzzled. Jehenna looked angry and scared. She kept shooting looks at Nanopoulos behind her back. I-Golem inched away from their conversation, by the will of four heaving, grunting, and cursing people. I couldn't make out words among all the signal noise, except for an occasional swear word. I popped a programming screen and tweaked the radio transmission band up and down a microscale, trying to improve Golem's reception.

"This thing weighs a ton," someone said finally, through a steady avalanche of gravel on tin.

Half a ton, actually. I resisted saying it, of course. I canceled the screen and focused Golem's hearing on the captain and Jehenna.

". . . appreciate the offer," Jehenna said, "but it's unnecessary."

". . . just . . . can't make sense of . . . doing . . . crazy like this."

"She's a lowlife . . . trying . . . advantage."

A lowlife, huh?

"But what about the other man?" someone standing close to me-Golem asked. "The one who ran toward the pool?"

The man who spoke was the guest I-Golem had handed the gun to.

Jehenna shrugged. ". . . accomplice. Listen, Captain . . . we can handle . . . Aunt Rachel . . . situation under control. No real harm . . . I doubt . . . press charges. . . ."

Nanopoulos was still frowning. Then she sighed. "Very well. . . . good-byes and get going . . . Call the local precinct . . . statement." She paused. ". . . circumstances, perhaps . . . cancel . . . the wake."

Jehenna looked shocked. Her voice carried over the line noise. "That would be unheard of! Aunt Rachel would never think of such a thing!"

They shoved me-Golem up against the outer railing by the elevator. By this time Nanopoulos was walking away.

"When . . . communications problem . . . ?" an Oriental woman asked. Several other guests gathered there nodded and made noises. ". . . can't be out of . . . with the office . . ."

"It'll take a few hours to complete our media sweep," Jehenna replied in a raised voice. A groan went up. She added with a soothing gesture, palms down, "I'll make a general announcement upstairs in the first-floor atrium, if you'll all join me up there in a moment. We'll make arrangements for everyone to have access to a house phone.

"You don't want pictures and videos of all your actions here appearing on the nets, do you? Please bear with us while we ensure your privacy and safety."

While the guests dispersed, one of the guards pointed at me-Golem and asked a question I-he couldn't hear over the line noise. I popped the screen and tweaked the reception again.

". . . thousand-dollar bonus for the . . . finds Sidra," Jehenna was saying. She tossed one of the guards a set of keys. ". . . elevator down and . . . locked at the . . . Aunt Rachel arrives."

The guard caught the keys, salaamed, and pressed the elevator button. .

"Where's Ahmed?" she asked the others.

". . . Tim . . ." one of the guards said. "Looking for him."

Him had to be Sidra. So he'd gotten away and was in hiding somewhere. That was something, at least.

The bad reception was maddening and I had learned what I needed to know, so I disengaged and pried the beanie off my beanjack. I found that I had collapsed on my side and drooled on the tile.

A faint memory led me to a locker room along the walkway by the stairwell, which I managed to duck into without being noticed. I took an ultra-hot shower, shampooed and soaped down real good, trying not to enjoy the rare luxury too much—without a great deal of success.

When I stepped out of the shower, a full-length mirror on the bathroom door showed me to myself. Maybe it was how I'd rescued Rachne from Vetch all on my own, or how I'd stood up to Melissa, or the climb I'd just pulled off, or maybe it was a whole lot of things. But I looked different to my eyes. Better. A little too thin, maybe, and my tits weren't much, but even all bruised and scratched like I was I looked much better than that jelly interview had made me look.

A smile spread across my image's face. I ran my hands over my body and then hugged myself. You're OK, Ruby, I thought. You look good.

I put on a terry-cloth robe from one of the hooks. With the headset tucked inside, I tied the belt nice and snug. Then I ditched my gauze tatters in the trash cycler.

Lotions! On the washbasin counter. I hadn't noticed them, going in. And not the bargain-basement stuff that comes in plastic gallon jugs, either: the impossibly expensive stuff that appears in ghost hands of gorgeous models in the jello-tube. With piles of soft cotton pads and cloths for application and removal. And cremes and powder puffs, perfumes, and cosmetics. All in etched crystal bottles and glass bowls glossed with metal oxides, lined up on the basalt-topped dressing table in front of a mirror whose surface was gilt with gold. And paints and kohls for the eyes and face in miniature vials of cut glass—and sparkle dust, and chime skin.

I sat down in one of the velvet-cushioned saddle stools, picked up bottles, sniffed and dabbed, smudged streaks of shimmer creme colors on the backs of my hands, on my arms and thighs to hide all the scrapes and bruises I'd gotten fighting Vetch and coming across on the strut. I rubbed cremes onto my eyelids and face, carefully disguising my now black eye and the gouge on my cheekbone. I dipped a finger in the chime skin, and snapped my fingers. Tiny bells whispered, far away—a sigh of high, clear notes.

Once done, I scrutinized myself. Much better. And well disguised, in case someone had seen my face in the nets. I put the beanie back on and turned off the Golem-input, for the moment. With expensive cremes sparkling and chiming on my face, arms, and thighs and my head turbaned in a towel, I was just another Jacuzzi-soaked houseguest.

Moxie, Ruby. Avoid Nanopoulos and remember your moxie. I strolled out of the locker room with a smile and a nod at the woman heading in. She smiled and nodded back. So far, so good.

A pair of male guards had stationed themselves in the pool area, eyeing the nude bodies. I entered the pool area and, heart banging so loud I was sure they could hear it, reclined in a chaise longue by the pool. A server gave me a flute of champagne with a strawberry floating in it, buoyed up by bubbles.

Champagne—and a strawberry. A real strawberry. This was as close as I was ever going to get.

I took a mouthful of the champagne; it was sour and effervesced like Alka-Seltzer. Cool fire burned my sinuses going down. I suppressed a cough. The second mouthful went down more smoothly. The taste clung to my tongue, in a way I decided I liked.

Then I dug the strawberry out with my fingers. It was real, a real strawberry. My mother had told me about them. I ate it in tiny bites, lingering over it, remembering my mother and what she said things used to be like and feeling sad. The fruit was sweet and delicious; I licked red, pulpy juice from my fingers and then took a last swallow of champagne. Reluctantly, I put the drink down.

I picked up an e-mag lozenge on the table next to me and popped it into the display unit mounted on the chair arm. I watched the ad displays and interviews in the glass cylinder for a couple of minutes for camouflage. The ads were the most amazing part—all slick, all artful flash and allure. Watching them, I felt like I had when Melissa had kissed me: lusty, and dirty. Ashamed. Knowing as they seduced me who was doing the screwing and who was getting screwed. Then I laid the e-mag, still running, on my chest and closed my eyes.

The baroque music coming from the guitar-bot, the bitter oily smoke from the torches and floating candles tickling my nose, the aroma of the perfumes I'd donned—even the tastes of champagne and fruit lingering in my mouth—were all intensely distracting. But after a moment or so I was able to climb up out of my body and down into Golem's.

I-Golem retracted his arms and dropped to all fours, scanning. Some people stood talking far down the walkway to the north; I-he zoomed on them. They looked harmless, simply a couple of guests admiring the view, but you never know. I-he started toward the south. Then Sidra climbed over the railing, right over the glowing sign that said DANGER! DO NOT CLIMB OVER RAILING OR STEP ON METAGLASS!

He saw me-Golem and froze with one leg over the railing.

"Oh, wait, wait right there," I-Golem said.

I disengaged from Golem, got to my feet and walked in a controlled panic past the guards, burst through the double set of glass doors. The scent of earth, leaf, and blossom rose up on a fountain of cold air, headier and more wholesome than the bottled ointments I wore. I sped around the curve of the gardens, clutching my robe and towel turban.

When I rounded the curve Sidra was gone. I spun around, hissed his name—then leaned over the railing. There he was, lying spread-eagled on the clear surface. He looked up at me.

"Hi," I said. "I'm Ruby. You've already met my waldo."

He whispered something that might have been a curse and his body convulsed—a sigh, maybe, or a laugh or sob. I went over and knelt next to Golem, opened his compartment, unlocked the secret safe, and pulled out the envelope.

I-Golem reared and backed over against the railing. Then I returned to myself and looked around. No one in sight. I climbed over the railing and slipped down to the floor beside Sidra. Between my feet, miniature boats bobbed in the wind far below. It made my toes hurt.

"Metaglass is a lot stronger than glass," I whispered, squatting next to him. The reminder was as much for myself as for him. "You can get up."

"What do you want from me?" His voice had a hysterical edge to it.

Footsteps came from different directions overhead, met a short distance away.

"What was that you said?" a voice asked.

"I didn't say anything."

"Any luck?"

"Naw."

"Need a light?"

"Thanks."

A flint was struck; the flare briefly lit up the leaves overhead. A pair of hands appeared over the edge of the rail; I pulled my feet in. A puff of blue smoke flowed out near the hands, and another set of hands appeared, one of which held a cigarette. The smell of burning tobacco reached us. I looked at Sidra; his eyes were wide.

"What miserable timing," one of the voices said. "My feet are killing me."

"Yeah, I already worked a double shift today. All these damned celebs. Julia's going to be flamed."

"Not if you bring home that ten-thousand-dollar bonus. I'm sure not going off-shift till I find him."

"Not if I find him first!"

Laughter. The cigaretteless hands disappeared. "We'll link up later."

"Later."

One set of footsteps faded. After a couple more puffs, the cigarette, still smoldering, flew through the air and landed on the glass among green leaves. The hands disappeared.

A vacubrush robot came across the floor toward us, whirring, and picked up the cigarette. We started up for the railing in alarm; then it veered aside and sped off, sucking up leaves and bird droppings.

We sat back down. Neither of us said anything until the footsteps had faded away.

"I'm getting out of here," Sidra finally whispered. "I'll thank you to go your own way and stay out of my life."

I touched his arm. "Look. I'm on your side, pal."

He gave me a suspicious look.

"Think for a minute. Why do you think they're holding you here? I have the only existing copy of your father's last will and testament, and Rachel doesn't want you to have it. *Think about it.*"

I handed him the gelpaper envelope. "Look in the envelope. I have your dad's cross. Where would I have gotten that if not from him? Where would I have gotten his earrings? Don't you see?"

He upended it, and the note, will, diamonds, and cross fell to the glass.

He picked up the will and note, read the note again. Then he picked up the cross, held it up, looked at the bronze martyr hanging from the tiny bronze nails, rubbed it between his fingers. His face was passionless. I didn't say anything.

"You could have robbed him," he said. "You could have stolen them off his body. That's how."

My tongue got glued to the roof of my mouth and my heart thumped against my rib cage. I just looked at him for a minute. Then I released a breath.

"Yeah. I robbed him. But I didn't make up the note, or the will or the cross. Those are yours. Straight from him to you."

Sidra looked at me. I nodded. He read the note again, shaking his head and frowning hard. Then he lifted the cross and chain and lowered it over his head. His head sank over his knees.

"Dad. I'm sorry. I'm sorry."

He started to sob, hoarse and awkward, like a man who hasn't cried often in his life. I just sat there, feeling embarrassed, while he choked and coughed out his grief. It seemed like forever. His eyes were all swollen and bloodshot when he looked up at me.

"I didn't want to believe you."

I didn't get it, but didn't tell him so. I wished I had a hanky to loan him because his nose was running. He stopped crying after a while and looked at the will with loathing.

"It was never the money," he said. "I never wanted his stupid money. I just wanted him to stop trying to force me to be a little Youhanna. . . ." His voice trailed away and memories played behind his eyes. "He could never accept me the way I was."

Tears started trickling down his face again as he fingered the cross, but he wasn't sobbing anymore. I couldn't tell if that was good or bad. Truth was, I was getting restless to get going, but the man deserved a little time to absorb it all.

He started crawling around on his knees, gathering the diamonds together. I gave him a hand.

"I remember when he bought this pair," he told me, holding up the smallest pair. "I was eight. He loved diamonds. Diamonds especially."

"Look," I said. "We have to get you out of here. I have a friend waiting in a collocopter across the river. He's expecting us up on the roof."

He sat oblivious, looking at the diamonds.

"Sidra. I need you to help me think, because I don't know this mansion. I can't get us out of here without your help. I don't think they have many security people on duty, but they have all the exits covered. There are also two guards by the pool so we can't take that stairwell. Where's the nearest access to the roof?"

He took a breath and forced his eyes to focus on me. "Call me Sid." Then his brow furrowed. "It's been a long time. But I think there's another stairwell on the north side of the gardens."

"Come on," I said.

ODE TO JIMMY-JACK

GOLEM had to carry me in his Flexbind web, and I never had such a time staying in his head. I-he clattered up the stairs in noisy jerks and starts that made Sid turn and glare at me. Half of the time I stared up the steps with Golem's cameras; the other half I got an eyeful of his psychedelic chassis with my own vision, bumping my nose and elbows on him as he jerked yet again to a halt.

I was terrified that one of those times he'd end up too far off balance for the programming to compensate, and he'd fall—crushing me like the old man had been crushed. Matters weren't helped by the fact that the stairwell was a furnace, and I had a hard time breathing in the confines of the webbing.

Golem and I fell far behind Sid. Finally I put Mikey's earphone headset on, and it helped a little.

Sid sat dripping sweat on the seventh-floor landing, his feet on the last step of the stairway around the corner when Golem and I caught up to him. The stairs continued to Sid's right. To his left, down a short hallway, was a door labeled with a big black 7.

Sid looked down at Ruby-me and me-Golem with despair in his eyes.

"What?" I asked, struggling to sit up in the webbing. He gestured at the stairs that continued up. I-Golem rolled over around the corner.

There was a metal door with large, shiny black letters painted on it: EMERGENCY ENTRANCE ONLY. ALARM WILL SOUND. At the top of the door was a red box and a Klaxon, with what must have been a magnetic switch.

"Security measure," he said. "I forgot about it. The family quarters are on the eighth floor. If we go through the door the alarm will go off."

"Does the other stairwell have this?"

"Yes."

"Are there any other ways up to the roof?"

He shook his head.

I thought for a moment, eyeing the door. "Is it locked?"

"No. Does it need to be?"

Ignoring the sarcasm, I scrambled out of Golem's webbing and climbed up his back, swinging my legs over to sit on his vidi platform. I inspected the alarm with my fingers and eyes.

"I wish I had my tools," I said. "I could jimmy this in a second flat."

Sid looked thoughtful. "Perhaps we can find some tools in Maintenance."

"Where are they?"

"Beneath the recreations area."

I wrinkled my nose. "All the way back down? Yuck."

Then my glance fell on Golem's snake arm that hung coiled like a whip at his side, and I remembered all those jimmy-jacks and what the user's manual said the warrior arm was able to do.

Sid demanded, as a grin spread across my face, "What? What is it?"

I scrambled back down into the webbing, adjusted my beanie, and activated the linkware.

"Sid," I-Golem said, "get ready to be impressed."

They always tell you to read the manual. I almost never bother. But this time discretion seemed in order, so I did it by the book.

Using the window in Golem's new camera eye, I dumped the manual into active memory and searched the topic list. Found it first try. *ALARM, magnetic, disarm.* Some hacker genius had written a macro.

The macro made it easy. Following instructions on the menu that hung in space in front of me, I-Golem unfurled the snake arm and installed it with the fittings listed. I-he did ultrasonic soundings on the alarm box itself and fed the readings into the software at the right prompts, then squeezed and shrank the resulting schematic over the actual box until it appeared to have a skeleton of red lines inside it. Little blue *X*'s flashed where I-he was supposed to drill holes.

After that it was simply a matter of plugging the recommended jimmy-jacks and miniature splicing tools in through the holes and using the schematic projection to find and cut into the optronics threads inside the box.

The connections closed. I-he left the spliced threads in place at the box, and dislodged and refurled the snake arm.

"That should do it," I-Golem said. I-he gripped the door bar with my finger-hander and exchanged a look with Sid.

"Ready?"

Sid gave me-Golem a single, sharp nod. I-he

pushed. With a metallic clank, the catch opened. Sid and Ruby-I drew sharp breaths. Silence . . .

Sid grinned at Ruby-me through the webbing; I grinned back. He came up behind as I-Golem pushed the door open. At that instant the Klaxon started to bellow, *ah-OOO-ga, ah-OOO-ga*, jerking me back to myself in time to go eye-to-camera with the mechanical monster bumping down the stairs toward us.

JUNGLE JIM,
REVISITED

I-GOLEM snatched Sid up with the snake arm, ground the gears into reverse, shot the telescope arm out as we fled backwards on the landing. From a good two meters away I-he grabbed the door's handle and contracted the arm toward me-him, yanking the door open in time for us to dodge through.

Corridors lay straight ahead, to the right, and to the left. I-Golem went straight. The door banged open behind.

"Tiny Tim," Sid panted, dangling before my-Golem's face, a human-sized rag doll. And, "I'm not impressed."

"Guess I should've ordered the software update."

I-Golem stopped at a large metal cabinet set against the railing, placed Sid on Golem's back, and wrapped the finger-hander around him.

"Hold tight," I-he said. Sid's only reply was a grunt.

The alarm still sounded, less ear-shattering but loud enough to draw the attention of guests, secu-

rity personnel, and house staff, who were pointing
and staring at us, leaning out along the balconies.
Beyond the railing. were the upper reaches of the
hanging garden. A cascade of vines with white flowers tumbled down a woven trellis, down and outward. Huge pots hung overhead, spilling waxy leaves
and penile yellow and red flowers.

Tiny Tim skated toward us on its five roll-step
legs. It was half again as massive as Golem, though
not as tall. Three triple-jointed arms bracketed its
stocky torso, with nasty sharp things for "hands,"
and an automatic weapon of some kind was
mounted beneath its vidi platform. The stereo-
scopic cameras were mounted on a long, skinny
multijointed neck.

Tiny Tim was coming up too fast to stop before
colliding with me-Golem; we'd be crushed against
the railing, or knocked over the edge. I-he could have
dodged, but I had a better idea.

I-Golem bent forward over the metal cabinet, retracted his wheels and extended the auxiliary
wheels, and edged myself-him off over the railing,
checking my grip on Sid as he asked, "What the hell
are you doing?" and someone below us screamed.

Tiny Tim slammed into the cabinet and knocked
us all the way off. One hundred feet down lay a
sheet of glass, and below that a four-hundred-foot
fall to the river.

Golem's telescope arm snagged the trellis three
meters out as we fell; we swung into it in a descending arc, and were showered with vine leaves and
sour-smelling white petals as we struck. Birds exploded into flight around us. The impact knocked
the wind out of me.

Sid cursed, pawing around Golem's chassis to
shake me in my FlexBind webbing. "You'll kill us!"

I opened my eyes to look at him, drew in an over-due breath. "I've got news for you. Tiny Tim is the one trying to kill us. They want us both dead."

He didn't say anything. I-Golem did a fast scan as I-he started down the trellis, and pointed with the snake arm. "Look down."

That was no doubt the wrong thing to say. Turning deep forest-green, Sid squinted, but human eyes not having zoom lenses, he couldn't spot Nanopoulos at the railing at the first floor of the atrium below.

"Captain Nanopoulos of Manhattan's First Precinct police force is watching. We get to her before Tiny Tim up there stops us and we're safe."

I remembered what Mikey had suggested and how I'd passed up the opportunity to be arrested before. Having your life endangered certainly puts a different perspective on things.

"Captain Nanopoulos? *Sheila* Nanopoulos?"

"The very same."

He frowned, but said nothing. I-Golem tightened my grip on him.

"Relax," I-Golem said, scrambling across and dropping to a pot with a giant spider plant. It swung, a ponderous pendulum, and the floor below twisted sickeningly. "I've done this sort of thing a thousand times."

I didn't bother to mention that I'd never done it with myself as a passenger before, and that I was as terrified as he was.

Golem's weight in combination with ours was pushing the tolerances of the hangings. They creaked, groaned, and snapped around us. I-he moved out toward the far end of the garden so the security people couldn't sneak up on us. They ringed the balconies, four or five per floor, with weapons trained. So far they were holding their fire.

"Heads up," Sid said, and I saw that Tiny Tim had gotten over the railing and was descending toward us.

Tim the security waldo didn't have a telescope extension—it used a cord function instead, fired the cord like spider's thread and slid along it, landed, retracted the cord, and fired as it sprang into the air again. That fucker was *fast*.

"Shit." I-Golem checked my grip on Sid and jumped.

That piece of equipment might be a decade's worth of higher tech than Golem, but it wasn't any more designed for climbing than Golem was. And I was willing to bet the pilot didn't have my years of experience climbing in high-hazard, low-stability conditions.

Using Golem's three free arms, flipping upside down, over, right-side up, like a mechanical gorilla, I-Golem swung down further. All the twisting started to give Ruby-me motion sickness.

I-he moved behind a wall of ferns and flowers and deposited Sid in a row of Boston ferns and English ivy, out of sight of the balconies.

"Keep down."

Sid nodded, hunched down as low as he could. Lightning flashed outside the sheet of metaglass; thunder boomed, and rain pounded the wall. He gave me a thumbs-up as I-Golem swung away.

I-Golem climbed the supports as fast as I-he possibly could, keeping obstacles between Tiny Tim and me-Golem whenever possible. Something whizzed past—an explosion concussed in my chest and ears—glass spewed outward from the wall, a shower of gleaming shards. Tiny Tim was on my-

Golem's level, and coming fast, bringing the mini-cannon to bear.

Pushing out from a pot, I-Golem fell—another exploding shell ripped by overhead, turned the pot to ceramic shrapnel. Ruby-I took pottery splinters in the back. I-Golem shoved against a rafter with the snake arm, rolling to put Ruby-me on top—crashed through the branches of a bush, grasping at the branches with the schwarzenegger and the finger-hander to slow my-his fall.

With the telescope arm I-he caught a rope and contracted the arm; the fall became an arc, which carried me-Golem back up almost to Tiny Tim's level. I-he snagged a pot support line, and hung on while the viny rope fell away.

Jehenna was shouting from the balcony a floor below. I realized belatedly she was telling someone named Ahmed to lay off with the shells. Must have been Tiny Tim's pilot.

Tiny Tim was having difficulties; it had crashed through a rope trellis and now struggled, snarled in a mass of vines and cords, thrashing about and crushing orchids on a planter just above me-Golem, several meters closer to the balcony. The wires and ropes holding the planter groaned with the added weight.

I-Golem swung and scrambled over to directly beneath the planter, then scrambled up on top. The other waldo focused on me-Golem and Ruby-me. I opened my own eyes and looked at it, shuddered, and maneuvered Golem around so Ruby-I was more protected. I-he reached up and grabbed hold of the support wires with two hands, popped open his chassis, extracted the wire-cutter fitting.

Tiny Tim made a *gaakk* noise; one of its three arms swiped at me-Golem, rocking the planter and nearly knocking me-us off. That pissed me off. I-he drove the snake arm like a pile driver into the waldo's side beneath that arm, and whipped the edge about inside with the splicing razor while yanking on the arm with the schwarzenegger. Tiny Tim's arm came free with a metallic shriek and I-he tossed it over the side.

Not a good tactical move. The snake arm had cut through some of the entangling cords on its way in and Tiny Tim was that much closer to having both remaining arms free. Time for desperate measures.

I-Golem cut Ruby-me free of the webbing; cold metal arms cradled me. I-Golem pressed the wire cutter into Ruby-my nerveless hands. Then Ruby-I fell up, up—and I caught hold of the cording, dug feet and hands in. I bent over and sawed away at the wires buried in the woven cords—while Golem stood lifeless and defenseless two meters below me, and the half-ensnarled security waldo struck at him, blow after blow.

A wire gave suddenly, with a melodic twang, and ripped a gash up my arm. One corner of the planter dipped—Golem toppled. Instantly I was in him, scanning. A draping vine trellis caught me-him two floors down, bending the telescope arm; I-he rolled and grabbed at the rope trellis, slowing his fall. With a crunch, I-he landed in a jade plant. I locked him there and returned to myself.

Wiser, perhaps, to have let him go; Tiny Tim was now after me. Only its legs were tangled now, and it didn't need those to climb. It had started up one of the supports toward me, and I was staring right into the black hole of its minicannon. If the pilot got crazy I'd eat a shell point-blank.

"Hold your fire, Ahmed!" Jehenna screamed. "Hold your fire!"

I prayed he heard her, prayed he'd obey. You never did see a woman chop at a wire so hard in your life.

Tiny Tim's next swipe nearly broke my right foot. It went numb. I was too junked on adrenaline to feel any pain. I clawed my way up the cording with two hands and the other foot, barely out of the waldo's reach—chopped and hacked at the wires with trembling, bloody hands. Where had the blood come from?

Another wire gave, then another. More cording collapsed on top of Tiny Tim. The planter dangled from a single support. Tiny Tim flailed and slipped, then, reentangled, it fell. Smashed through a planter ablaze with red, white, and yellow tulips. And fell. And fell. And shattered clay pots going down like a mallet striking dirt clods. And fell.

Tiny Tim struck the metaglass flooring—and to my amazement *bounced*, rose a good eight or ten meters through the tons of falling plant debris and dirt and pottery shards, arms flailing, and then dropped again. This time the metaglass shattered with a sound like a rifle shot, and the waldo tumbled downward, trailed by a rain of glass and potting soil. My ears crackled; hot air rushed up and I broke into an instant sweat.

A vacubrush bot sped to the fracture, sucking dirt, and plummeted over the edge after the waldo. Then a second. A third. A fourth. Mechanical lemmings.

I downloaded into Golem and zoomed to track the waldo's fall. Tiny Tim plummeted, followed by its imitators, down past the river elevator: a lozenge of white brilliance rising in the column of glass like a bubble in honey-colored liquid. At maximum zoom I-Golem could see who was in the elevator.

Rachel, her head dropping to track the waldo's descent, gaped at the shower of robots and broken

glass. With her were Vetch and, huddled against the
elevator wall with her arms folded about her and
looking miserable, Melissa.

WHERE THERE'S
A WILL . . .

BY the time I-Golem had gotten Sid and Ruby-me
down out of the hanging gardens—a task made more
difficult not only by the damage Golem had sustained but by the fact that I was now feeling the
abuses my body had taken and had a hard time staying in Golem's head—Captain Nanopoulos was nowhere in sight.

House security types descended on us like a horde
of yellow jackets. I was in no condition to run, dripping blood from my back, hands, and arms and unable to put weight on my right foot. Sid put an arm
around my waist to help me stay upright and I
looked about anxiously for the police captain.

They threatened us with weapons, took my
beanie, and escorted Sid and me through the crowd
of ogling guests into the kitchen, through a cloud of
mouth-watering aromas. I realized it had been almost a full day since I'd eaten.

They chased the Brooklyn chef and his assistants
out—not without a string of loud protests about
what would happen to the soufflés without him
there to keep an eye on them—and took us to a
small room behind the kitchen with a walk-in
freezer, pantries, table, and two industrial-sized alu-
minum sinks. Two guards posted themselves inside
the swinging doors.

Sid and I sat down at the waxed wood table, amid barbecued sides of pork and strings of papery onions. I leaned forward—my back was aflame from the shards imbedded in it. I smelled smoked pork, onion, pastries, and burning soufflés. My stomach growled. It sounded like grinding gears.

They hadn't searched us yet, but when they did, Sid's will would fall right into their hands. I gave him a look of dismay. He returned a wan smile that was probably meant to be reassuring.

Two women came in with Mikey handcuffed between them. They made him sit down and then joined the other two guards at the door. Mikey looked even more rumpled than usual, and in serious need of a toothpick.

"Hey, Ruby."

"Mikey—"

"Were all them explosions and the falling waldo and things your doing?"

I broke into a grin despite myself. "I guess so."

"Huh. I figured if all that weren't a signal nothing was."

"Your bird—?"

He jerked his chin up. "Roofward."

"You flew over and landed in this storm?" Sid asked.

Mikey gave him a sheepish grin. "Well, it got a little bumpy. Nothing serious. Hell, it was kind of exhilarating."

"Sidra Nasser," I said, "meet my good friend Michael Cisneros Knowles. A.k.a. Mikey. Mikey, Sid."

They gave each other a nod.

Rachel strode in with Jehenna and a security man on her heels. I recognized him as the hologram who'd been speaking to Jehenna earlier. Ahmed. No doubt he was not too happy with me at the moment.

Following them were Melissa and Vetch. I tried to stand, collapsed with a gasp when my foot gave out.

"You OK?" I asked Melissa. I'd already made up my mind to ignore Vetch. She gave me a weak smile, pushed Vetch's arm away and moved toward me.

I glared at Rachel. "You have no right—"

"Shut up." She turned to the guards. "Search all three. Thoroughly."

They did Mikey, then me, then Sid. I fought them, which was stupid, given my exhaustion, the bleeding back, wire-sliced condition of my hands, and damaged foot. Not to mention that—unlike Sid—I had nothing to hide. It was just the indignity of it.

They left me in a heap on the floor with a few extra bruises and dumped the filthy, riddled terry-cloth robe in my lap. I struggled back into it and gave a look of terror to Sid.

He stood, naked, arms outstretched, with his robes at his feet, while the guards went over him. There were secrets behind his eyes and dignity in his stance. There was no cross about his neck. Ahmed turned to Rachel.

"Nothing."

"Then disassemble the collocopter and that—heap of junk in the atrium. I'm certain she brought it with her," she said, with a glance at Melissa and Vetch.

That glance said everything. If Vetch hadn't been there I could have told myself Melissa had been captured and forced to tell her. But I knew better. She'd betrayed me. With a little encouragement from Vetch and Rachel, she'd sold my love for cash.

Melissa knelt next to me, pressed her hands

against my cheeks. I caught a glimpse of Vetch behind her, Jehenna and Rachel behind him.

"Give her what she wants, honey," Melissa said. "It's no good. Give her what she wants and let's go home."

I pulled Melissa's hands away from my face and met Rachel's gaze, avoiding a glance at Sid. He must have hidden the envelope somewhere, in the hanging gardens perhaps.

"Surely you don't think I'd be stupid enough to bring it with me," I said, trying not to wince. And it had seemed like such a good idea at the time. "I have it in a safe deposit box, with instructions for it to be opened unless I call them within the next eight hours."

Rachel gave me a disgusted look. "You're lying."

Damn, I wished I lied better.

After studying me a moment, though, her expression changed. I wondered what she thought she saw in my face. "It'd be worth a lot to me to have that will. I'll make it worth your while to cooperate."

Melissa looked at me, pleaded with her eyes, dug her fingers into the palms of my hands, which still clung to hers.

"Name your price," Rachel said. "Anything."

I pulled my hands free of Melissa's and shook my head. It wasn't even mildly tempting. Mikey and I shared a look, and Sid gave me a smile. I shook my head at Rachel again.

"Lady, you don't deal in the right kind of currency. No way."

"You won't find it," Sid said.

Rachel glanced at him and something ugly flickered in her eyes. Her lips curved up.

"I needn't find it. If I'm right that she brought it with her—and I am—I need merely to suppress it."

He shook his head as if in wonderment. "And you claim to have loved him."

Her face drained of color, as though he'd struck her. Her voice came out low and even. "For fifteen years he tried to forget the grief and shame you brought him. Fifteen years I watched, helpless, while he struggled to recover from the blow you dealt by abandoning him and his God.

"I prayed he'd find peace, forget the son who'd flung all his love and hopes in his face. He never did. He died with a bitter pain in his heart. Because of you. He went out that day before the storm, because of you. He'd be alive now, but for you. I despise you for the pain you caused him."

We all looked at Sid.

"Oh, climb off it. What you have is a case of ordinary greed. Stop hiding it behind your Mother Superior routine." Sid paused. "You know, he might have deserved better from me than he got, but he sure as God's green earth deserved better than you."

I had to cover my mouth to hide the grin that spread across it. Mikey winced.

Rachel tried to stare Sid down, but he didn't flinch. Then she looked around at us all, and she must not have liked what she saw, because she flicked a hand, encompassing Melissa, Mikey, Sid, Vetch, and me.

"Rid me of this problem," she said to Ahmed. I don't think anyone there mistook her intent.

Ahmed gestured at one of his guards, who opened the walk-in freezer door. Inside hung slabs of raw meat and beneath them, boxes stained with bloody drippings. I felt weird and disconnected, started to hear the distant screaming again.

Sorry, old man. Did all I could. Looks like I'm about to join you in spookville.

Melissa started to cry. Vetch grabbed Rachel's arm. "We had a deal!"

Rachel pried her arm free. A guard put a gun to Vetch's temple and he backed away, hands raised, pale and sick looking.

"We *had* a deal," Rachel said.

Jehenna looked after Rachel, stunned. "Aunt Rachel—surely it's not worth killing over—"

"Wait!" Sid said. "I'll give you the will."

Rachel ignored both of them and went out through the doors.

She came back in a second, following Captain Nanopoulos and six—no, eight—armed police officers. I think that was the first time in my life I was glad to see the police.

"This is totally uncalled for," Rachel was saying. "You have no warrant. You have no right—"

The captain handed her a sheet of glossy plastic. "I took the liberty of borrowing your facsimile machine, Rachel. One search warrant. Signed, sealed, and delivered."

Rachel scanned it. Her carmine-glossed lips went thin. "This isn't legal."

"I assure you it is. I'll have the DA refer you to the proper legal precedent later."

I couldn't help grinning. The cops spread through the room and disarmed the house security people. Nanopoulos looked down at me. For some reason I found her glance reassuring. Then she turned back to Rachel.

"Now," Nanopoulos said, speaking to Rachel, "I realize this is terrible timing; allow me to apologize in advance for any undue injury. But circumstances force me to put the professional before the personal. I want to know what's going on here."

We all started talking at once. Nanopoulos waved us to silence.

"Rachel?" she said.

Rachel composed herself. "The search warrant was unnecessary, Sheila. In fact, I'm glad you're here. My stepson is apparently attempting to harm me; he has hired these hooligans"—with a gesture at the rest of us—"to break in and vandalize my house during the wake. I want to press charges to the fullest extent of the law."

Mikey, Melissa, Vetch, and I all broke out in protests. Nanopoulos waved us to silence again.

"Sidra?" she said. "Is that what has happened?"

Sid shook his head. "No, Aunt Sheila, it isn't. With your permission, I'd like to retrieve something from the hanging gardens. I believe it'll explain a lot."

A Parting of Ways, Take Two

"I was so scared for you, honey," Melissa said. She'd been giggling, babbling, and pacing for over an hour. It was infuriating, and pitiful.

I sat sipping at a cup of scalding, bitter kaffe, favoring my seal-patched back and hands and my foot with its baby-blue, plastic splint, and looked out through the chicken wire at the lighted street. I was riding a neuro-designer painkiller high, a meter or so above my body, and occasionally I glanced back at Melissa, wondering what she'd had or been that had so filled me with lust and need.

"That's why I went to meet her at the train station," she went on. "To protect you. To protect us. It was Darian's idea about the money, really. I just wanted to make sure you didn't get hurt."

Pace. Giggle.

"She's crazy, you know? She was actually going to kill us."

She shivered, hugging herself, and fear moved in her eyes. She sat down next to me, touched my knee. I shifted away.

"You're being so quiet, Rube. It's not like you. Are you angry with me?"

I searched her face, searched in myself for a spur of anger, a lump of pain at her betrayal. Nothing. Except sadness that she didn't have it in her to be more than she was, and sadness that I'd lost something by growing beyond my need for her.

It was time to stop making Melissa's problems my responsibility, and stop blaming her for all of mine. Time to move out and get a place of my own. There were others out there to love. There was a whole world out there and I'd been hiding from it for too long.

The sadness passed. Something felt right, deep down inside. The old man had given me some kind of gift, beyond his horrible death, beyond the pain. I felt ready to choose—not merely accept being chosen.

I smiled and gave her shoulder a comforting pat.

"I'm not angry with you, Liss," I said, and turned back to the window.

. . . There's a Way

Captain Nanopoulos wore pearl-rimmed crescent specs strung with a serpentine silver chain. Her gaze was austere when she looked over them at me, but I sensed warmth beneath it. I found myself wondering if she had any kind of permanent relationship, and felt a smile rise from inside. The idea bore exploring.

Nanopoulos gestured. "Sit down."

I sat in the chair before her desk, carefully, to avoid pain, and crossed the leg with the splinted foot.

"Charges of fraud, kidnapping, and attempted murder have been filed against Rachel and Jehenna Karam. Eventually I expect the DA's office will ask you to testify at their trials. That'll be a while down the road. You'll be notified when your contribution is needed."

I nodded. I wanted to ask whether she thought Rachel would be convicted, as powerful and wealthy as she was, but Nanopoulos probably didn't know the answer to that any better than I did.

She looked at a piece of paper on her desk. "Now. About those belongings of Dr. Nasser's you took. I've read your deposition, and discussed the matter with Sidra. He has decided to drop all charges of theft against you." She lifted the piece of paper, browsed it through her specs, looked up over the tops of them again. "Under the circumstances, I'm inclined to agree."

"Sidra—he's your nephew?"

She shook her head, and a sad little smile came and went. "I'm an honorary aunt. An old friend of the family. His mother and I were close."

"Where is Sid?"

Nanopoulos removed her glasses. "He left a short while ago. He asked me to extend his regrets that he wasn't able to thank you personally—many things suddenly require doing and he had to leave."

He didn't say good-bye. My throat closed. For some reason, that hurt far more than Melissa's betrayal.

"Does this mean I'm free to go?" I said, and came to my feet. "And Golem, too?"

"You are free to go. And Golem. I've arranged transportation for you and your waldo." She stood. "Ruby—"

"Has Mikey left yet?"

"He's outside, waiting for you. I believe your roommate and her boyfriend have already left. Wait—"

I turned, already at the door. She held out an envelope and a little black box. The box was vinyl, and had a gold-embossed H&H on the outside. My heart started pounding and my mouth went dry. I took it, opened it.

The largest pair of diamonds lay glittering among the folds of black velvet. In the envelope was a voucher for $250,000 made out to Mikey, and a messy scrawl from Sid.

> *Ruby,*
>   *I can never repay you for all you've done, but please accept these diamonds as a small token of my gratitude. Deliver the voucher to Mikey with my thanks for his help, too.*
>   *I'll call you soon.*
>   *Sid*

And so he did.

AUTHOR'S NOTE

THIS book had some midwives, body and soul, whom I want to mention with thanks.

Help with the Body

Dr. Richard T. Wetherald of Princeton University gave me loads of useful information on the predicted impact of the greenhouse effect, extrapolated from recent climatological models. He shared speculations on the possible effects of increasing greenhouse gases on storms, desert encroachment, ocean level rise, and food supply, all of which helped me flesh out my world.

My sister Kay Mixon, jeweler and artist, gave me advice on diamonds. My husband Steven Gould helped me with plotting and contributed some great ideas. Geary Rachel and Bob Stahl provided tips on electronics and computers that kept me from making egregious boo-boos, and Rory Harper, Martha Wells, and Terry Boren gave me useful writerly critiques. And Patrick Nielsen Hayden took a chance on me.

Help with the Soul

This story is about friendship, regrets, and unpaid debts, and at its heart are some relationships that have meant a lot to me.

Robin Matthews, who stood by me when there was no one else; I measure courage and loyalty by her example. Carol Pinkerton and Margaret Mauser, who taught me about creativity and intellectual bravery. Charlotte Vane, who showed me what music and spirituality are.

The class of Clarion 1981, teachers and fellow apprentices. My fellow Peace Corps trainees (P.S.—Jim Wold, the flowers were lovely). John Sigda—Sorry I wasn't honest with you. Irene Boczek, my first professional role model. Cynthia, I needed so much I didn't know how to ask for. I remember you with love.

And lastly, my cat Carli. That was a horrible death, Carli. Wish I could have saved you.